STRANGEST DAY SO FAR

An Eldritch Roads Novel

G V Pearce

First published by Improbable Press in 2020

Improbable Press is an imprint of:

Clan Destine Press
www.clandestinepress.com.au
PO Box 121, Bittern Victoria 3918 Australia

National Library of Australia Cataloguing-In-Publication data:

G V Pearce
Strangest Day So Far

ISBN: 978-0-6489586-4-2 (pb)
ISBN: 978-0-6489586-5-9 (eb)

Cover artwork by © Willsin Rowe

Design & Typesetting by Dimitra Stathopoulos

Improbable Press
improbablepress.co.uk

For Božena, Caitlin, and Cathy.
Never lend Mothman your chapstick, he won't give it back.

1

A CLOSE ENCOUNTER WITH A SURFACE-TO-AIR MISSILE IS GOING TO ruin anyone's day.

This is especially true when the person involved is strapped into a parachute harness, several thousand feet above enemy terrain, in the middle of the night.

For as long as he could remember, Ronan's personal philosophy had been 'you can't plan for everything, but you should still try to plan for anything.' That approach to life had saved his arse more times than he could count. Still, he'd always known the day would come when his plans reached their limit.

How unfortunate that he was reaching the limit here, of all places.

The early stages of the mission had been perfect.

If things had gone south before they'd even taken off, he wouldn't have been in this mess. If the attack had come while they were still in the helicopter, he'd at least have more options. If, if, if. That wasn't a useful thought.

A person could undo their life all the way back to childhood with wishes like that.

Ronan was aware that his thoughts were heading in entirely the wrong direction. That was understandable given that he was likely suffering from concussive injury and catastrophic blood loss, but understandable is not the same as helpful.

Then again, debating the merits of his own thoughts wasn't exactly helpful, either.

He wondered whether this was what dying felt like.

The missile had exploded on impact with something – or rather *someone* – else. Some unlucky member of his squad a few feet to his left whose identity had been hidden from him by the darkness.

The last he'd seen of them through the bright afterimages was burning scraps of parachute drifting away towards the stars.

From his own slightly erratic trajectory through the air he could tell his parachute was damaged, but not compromised. It wouldn't be worth the risk of switching to the auxiliary chute. Not at this height.

If there was no further gunfire the main parachute would get him to the ground.

Of course, there was more gunfire. He was in a war zone. No one ever fires a missile, then just walks away. The enemy knew for sure they were there now – the glow of the explosion would have highlighted their positions – and there was little they could do until they were on the ground. Not in the dark.

He had no idea how far they had left to fall – checking his altimeter would mean looking down.

Right now, he'd do anything to avoid looking down.

It wasn't just that he couldn't feel his legs.

He knew his weight was off.

Over the last few years he'd done hundreds of jumps, with varying amounts of equipment, so he knew exactly how his trajectory would be changed by a difference in weight.

Since the explosion he was moving as if he'd lost about fifteen kilos, but his pack and his weapons were still in place.

If he let his concentration slip, for just a moment, he knew he'd be able to feel the pain, somewhere in the region of his thighs.

He could not allow himself to do that.

Not at this altitude.

Not when he still had to get to the ground.

There would be time to consider the dim glow coming from his trousers and the smell of burning meat, but now was not that time.

In the near distance there was a second flash of a light from a hamlet that intelligence had sworn was unoccupied.

Time slowed.

Ronan's teeth rattled in his skull at the roar of another rocket as it passed him by.

Above and behind him something detonated, raining burning shrapnel on the soldiers it briefly illuminated, once again ruining the cover they'd hoped to gain from a night-time drop.

More lights, smaller this time, appeared around the roof of the tallest building. Tracer fire. The zip of bullets cutting the air a moment later. Concerned for his platoon, Ronan twisted in his harness, trying to see if any had been injured by the weapons fire. He barely noticed the first bullet tearing through his parachute. Or the second. The third forced his eyes upward when it compromised the structure enough for the parachute to finally fail. In the slowest of motions, the arch of fabric began to collapse.

Just as he reached for the cord to his reserve parachute, another light blossomed below. There was nothing he could do but instinctively cover his face when, seconds later, a third missile detonated far too close to him.

He was bowled through the air like a dandelion seed, the pain in his legs an indistinct white-hot mass that threatened to unhinge him.

The reserve wouldn't open.

His primary parachute would not detach, the lines tangled as the crumpled mass of fabric spun him dizzyingly through the air.

The ground was approaching too fast.

He wouldn't have enough stability to roll into the landing.

He didn't have enough time to try.

Major Ronan Cox hit the ground like a sack of bricks and was unconscious before his helmet met the sand.

The sky was still dark.

How long had he been laying in the dirt?

There were distant sounds of gunfire, explosions and shouts that could have been words if only he had the power to concentrate on them through the pain.

A man was perched on a nearby rock, watching him.

The man was naked. Winged and made of flames.

Ronan could hear helicopters to the south.

They wouldn't find him here if he didn't get their attention.

He tried to sit up. Fresh agony crackled up his sides each time he struggled to move his legs.

In the wavering glow of the man's burning wings Ronan could dimly see that his own thighs ended in a bloody twisted mess. His eyes refused to focus in the uncertain light, or perhaps that was just the effect of his head spinning.

He lay back and stared at the stars for a long moment as if they might help him think straight.

Wait.

What?

He turned his head to the side to look at the scene again.

Yep, that was a man. Made of fire. Or maybe it was a fire in the shape of a man. A man with wings. His gaze travelled down the man's chest of its own accord. Wow. A naked man, who really should put some trousers on.

Don't be ridiculous, his brain supplied in a faraway tone, he can't wear trousers – they'd just catch on fire.

Letting his eyes drift shut, Ronan wondered vaguely whether asbestos trousers would help.

If this was a hallucination, it was a strange one. He'd seen weirder things in his life that had turned out to be real – ignoring them was never a good idea. If the man wasn't real, well, at least Ronan wouldn't be bored while he died.

He should be doing something about the helicopters to the south.

He didn't have the energy to think of anything.

The man was speaking, using the crackle and hiss of the flames to blend together into words.

Through a mind filled with cotton wool Ronan did his best to recite the stock phrases he'd learned in case he met any friendly locals.

There was no point offending the man by assuming he was hostile. Ronan was incapacitated – if this creature meant to harm him, surely he would have done so by now.

The fire-being just looked confused.

Ronan continued for a few more words before he realized he was actually speaking Welsh instead of Arabic.

Welsh wasn't even his first language.

Now he couldn't remember what he'd been trying to say.

How bad was this head injury? The pain radiating up from his legs was overwhelming his senses to the point that he couldn't even tell whether his head hurt or not. He just wanted to sleep.

Giving up on speech, he went back to staring at the stars. He must have lost a lot of blood, but he didn't have the energy to do anything about that.

A hand waved in front of his face, trailing sparks.

What did this thing want, seeing that they couldn't communicate? Why didn't it just leave him there? The hand returned again, this time holding up three fingers.

Ronan raised an eyebrow.

"Ifrit don't grant wishes," he muttered, remembering an angry lecture he'd once received from a translator in Afghanistan. Strange that he could barely stay awake, but the creature's name had leapt to his tongue so easily.

More gestures he couldn't follow. A frantic flapping of fiery wings. Another crackling monologue. There was a lot of pointing, mostly at the ground just to the other side of Ronan's head, where the remains of his parachute lay crumpled and useless.

Gritting his teeth in anticipation of the pain, Ronan reached out and swept the fabric aside.

There were shards of pottery scattered amongst a mess of stones, a boot, and what looked like scraps of Ronan's uniform. He didn't look too closely at the boot, or its contents. That way madness lay.

The pottery had once been a brightly decorated vase or urn, aged by sun and sand to almost the color of the surrounding dirt. It had been smashed during his impact with the ground.

A fresh splatter of blood ran across a partial line of text that he couldn't read. Ah. Shit. Had he freed the being from some kind of bondage? Or had he unintentionally made a blood oath? Again?

He was too light-headed to care very much. Moving had been a mistake. The pain from his legs had receded to a bone-deep cold. Here he was in a desert, next to a man made of fire, and he'd never been so cold in his life.

He should sleep.

If he was asleep, he wouldn't notice the cold, or the way the stars whirled above him.

Sleep sounded like a wonderful idea.

The three fingers were back, inches from his nose, demanding attention by searing his face through their sheer proximity.

Wishes. He'd have to tell that guy in Afghanistan that he was wrong.

Ronan choked back a laugh. He wasn't going to live long enough to tell anyone anything.

What wishes could he make now?

The pain was gone, the world was following after. There'd be nothing left of him soon.

That thought didn't comfort him.

"I don't want to die here," he slurred, eyes still fighting to close. One finger folded against the creature's burning palm. "I don't want anyone else to die here." Another digit bent; one finger remained.

Ronan thought for a moment, vision fading in waves. "Are any of my troops wounded?"

A pause. A shake of the head. A cloud of sparks.

The sparks drifted up until they were lost amongst the stars.

"I..." He couldn't think. Anything beyond simple survival seemed both selfish and petty right now. "You keep the third wish. Use it for yourself. I wish you were free."

The remaining finger pointed emphatically toward the shattered vase. Oh, yes. The creature was already free. Ronan was far too tired to navigate this situation – he just wanted to sleep forever.

Something about the jagged pieces of pottery spoke to him.

"I don't want to be broken any more," he whispered, knowing full well that he didn't just mean his injuries, but too exhausted to understand what he actually meant.

The fiery hand folded into a fist.

Ronan's eyes finally closed.

Under the crackling of the fire he could hear the sound of helicopters growing louder.

Ronan had fallen asleep to pain and starry skies.

He woke to numbness and ceiling tiles.

Above him old stains crossed the suspended ceiling like a map to an undiscovered country. He would rather not consider their origins, but right now there was nothing else in his field of view.

Simply opening his eyes had felt like a struggle – turning his head was out of the question.

Somewhere to his right a deep voice was half-singing, half-muttering some melodramatic pop punk song at just the right volume to be impossible to ignore. Ronan did his best to shut it out – his brain already felt like it was firing at a tenth of its usual capacity.

If this was heaven, he'd been wildly misinformed. If it was hell, he was unimpressed. The devil was supposed to have more style than this. Which probably meant that – against all odds – he was alive.

He hadn't expected that outcome when he'd closed his eyes in the desert.

Now he wasn't sure what 'alive' was actually going to mean.

It took an effort of will just to feel the weight of his tongue in his mouth or the movement of his eyelids – anything about the rest of his body was still a mystery. He must have woke before some kind of anesthetic had properly worn off.

At any rate, he hoped that was the case.

Losing his legs was going to be bad enough. If he'd been paralyzed by the impact, too...

That thought slithered across his mind to leave a low-level panic in its wake. Like his body, his emotions felt weirdly detached, as if he knew his fear should be stronger but he couldn't reach it.

In a way, the fact that he wasn't feeling outright terror at the idea of paralysis supported his original conclusion – strong anesthetic would probably suppress his emotions as well as his senses.

Right now, he should probably focus more on where he was than worrying about what he could or couldn't feel.

During a brief pause in the singing – the voice stopped as if waiting out an unheard guitar solo – Ronan caught the beep of a heart monitor, and perhaps the distant sound of conversation. If he focused just enough, he could almost make out words.

Those sounds were lost again when the song resumed, and for the first time Ronan felt cool sheets as he clenched his fists in frustration. Oh, well, that meant his hands were coming back online. That had to mean something.

He let his eyes track slowly around the ceiling while he considered the new signals from his hands. There was a pastel-patterned curtain hanging from a railing to his left, and an empty railing to his right. Most of the artificial light, and the singing, was coming from that direction.

It was either night-time or there were no windows in this room.

There were wires clipped to his fingers and what felt like a cannula in the back of his hand. The afterlife was unlikely to need such mundane ways of monitoring him.

He was in a hospital. But where? Which military base?

Ronan tried to lift his shoulders to look around, but the movement was halted by a rush of nausea that soon turned to a burning pain in his throat. His teeth and jaw ached, too. He must have been intubated recently. The more he thought about the discomfort, the more it increased.

He turned his head, hoping that there would be water somewhere within reach, hopefully before the coughing fit he felt rising in his chest could properly take hold.

There was a plastic cup by the bed that seemed to glow with a heavenly light.

Well, he couldn't feel fear yet, but hyperbole was working just fine.

He couldn't get his arms to move properly.

Why was he alone? If he was coming around from a general anesthetic, why was no one there to monitor him?

Shuffling up enough to get one elbow under him took about as much effort as running up a flight of stairs. Freeing his other hand enough to reach the cup was even worse.

Once he'd finally got the drink, he found himself more or less stuck in place because his lower half still wasn't responding properly.

Now he was laid awkwardly on his side, facing into the bright glow of the lamp above the next bed, and unintentionally staring at that bed's occupant.

As far as views went – Ronan wasn't going to complain.

This was definitely an improvement on the ceiling tiles, or the plastic cup. The halo of lamp light didn't give the mystery singer much of a heavenly aspect, unless he was an angel who'd already fallen from grace.

Ronan should not be having thoughts like that about a complete stranger in a hospital bed.

He should have been thinking sensible things, like – who was he? Why was he here? Were his lips as kissable as they looked?

No.

Not appropriate.

Were they, though?

Well, he could safely say the anesthetic had worn off in the region immediately below his belt.

Ronan took another sip of water in hope of breaking his train of thought, but as long as he was stuck here staring at the man it was hard to think of anything else. As a bonus, he wasn't thinking about his throat anymore, so that was another positive.

The man in the next bed was quite possibly the least military-looking person Ronan could have imagined in that moment. Unless the military in question operated in some post-apocalyptic hellscape.

He was shirtless and his olive skin was covered in tattoos that were impossible to decipher at this angle.

One side of his hair had been shaved, the other was shoulder-length black curls. There were faded pink highlights around his face. It looked like the sort of artful mess that took an hour to achieve every morning.

His hair seemed to be deliberately arranged to show off his stretched earlobes and eyebrow ring. To continue that particular theme, Ronan could just see the telltale gleam of nipple piercings.

Well, one nipple piercing as far as Ronan could currently see. Tragically, the other side of his chest was covered in bandages. As was half of his face, although right now Ronan was finding it hard to stop looking at the exposed half of the man's torso long enough to even consider his face.

He had muscles for days: thick pecs and a washboard stomach; arms that Ronan knew he wouldn't be able to get both hands around; even the fingers jabbing at the cracked screen of his phone looked stronger that Ronan's whole body combined.

Ronan tried to lick his lips only to recoil at the sensation of his own sandpaper tongue.

The singing stopped abruptly.

"So, you're awake then," the man rumbled as he pushed back his headphones. The song continued as a soft tinny background hum.

A hot flush of embarrassment washed over Ronan when he realized he'd been caught staring, though the other man didn't seem to mind. In fact, when he finally made eye contact it was to wink.

He seemed to be wearing smudged eyeliner despite the bruising across much of his face. Ronan couldn't tell whether it had been added after the fact or just never washed away.

He looked thirty-something and his eyes were the warmest shade of brown Ronan had ever seen.

The blush returned for a second wave – he'd gone from staring at this stranger's chest to staring into his eyes.

"Well, *someone* was singing out of tune," Ronan snapped, trying to hide his embarrassment with anger.

Abruptly the man laughed, deep, loud, and unrepentant except for a small wince when his bandages pulled at his healing wounds. Despite that flash of pain his face almost glowed with his amusement. If Ronan had thought he was good looking before, he was stunning now.

God, what a prick, Ronan thought, why did he have to be stuck in a room with someone this beautiful and annoying?

"Aww you think I'm a beautiful prick?" the man crowed, laughing again in a way that made Ronan wonder what medication he was taking. "Wait 'til you see my cock!"

Oh no.

Ronan slapped a hand over his mouth, and wished the ground would swallow him whole. He'd just called this complete stranger a beautiful prick. It didn't matter what medication this guy was taking – what medication had *he* been given to end up saying something like that out loud?

To cover his mortification Ronan took a long drink and deliberately pushed himself fully upright so he was looking toward his own sheet-covered body.

Now the view was much less pleasant.

There was some kind of frame under the bed sheets, holding up the fabric over the space where his legs used to be.

The pain, fear, and stench of burning flesh all seemed to rush back at once. He wasn't in a half-lit room with a strange man watching him from the next bed; he was laying a pool of his own blood in the middle of a dark desert, with some nightmare creature made of fire standing over him as he died.

"Hey, do you need me to hit the call button? You don't look good," the man asked, his worried shape in the next bed nothing now but a pale blur at the edge of Ronan's vision.

Ronan wanted to look over at him – if only to let himself be distracted by muscles and dark eyes again – but he couldn't move. He felt like he could see through the fabric to the remains of his legs. But if he never looked, then he'd never have to face reality.

"Hey! Can you hear me?"

"Ye...yeah." He forced his head to turn towards the other man for a moment. "Yeah, I'm...I'll be fine."

The stranger's lips twisted into a sympathetic frown that struck Ronan as being far prettier than it had any right to be. His bottom lip had been split to one side and somehow the swelling made his mouth seem that much more kissable.

Which was, once again, an entirely inappropriate thought to be having, but it succeeded in snapping Ronan out of the dark mood that had just threatened to overtake him.

He recognized trauma well enough to know he shouldn't give in to the fear. Or the denial. Not looking wouldn't change anything. As long as he refused to accept what had happened, he wouldn't be able to heal.

Ronan clenched his jaw, ignoring the protests from his teeth where the tube had jostled them, and carefully tugged the blankets to one side.

There, on the bed, were his legs.

Both legs, still attached and whole all the way down to his feet.

Each one bore a long white adhesive dressing running from mid-thigh to half way down the shins he should no longer possess. His skin was horribly bruised, and there were dozens of smaller shrapnel wounds closed with stitches or tape, but there was no sign of the devastation he'd seen in the desert. No burns. No exposed bone.

He still had his legs.

The room was wavering around him, consumed by a fog that crackled with his own heartbeat.

This had to be a dream.

There was no way he still had his legs.

This was a cruel, evil dream.

Maybe he was still in surgery. Or he was still in the desert and the man in the next bed was just another hallucination.

Perhaps he was already dead.

Suddenly the idea that this was hell didn't seem all that unbelievable.

Somewhere in the distance he heard the sound of a buzzer, but he couldn't focus on it. This reality, and all its lies, were slipping away from him again.

2

HIS LEGS WERE MADE ENTIRELY OF FIRE.

He could feel each individual flame licking around shattered bones and the pulp that had once been his muscles. The fire crackled, hissed, and spat as it consumed the ruined mess the missile had left behind. He could smell his boots burning, his uniform burning, his skin, his tendons, his bone marrow – everything charring and twisting under the onslaught of this otherworldly conflagration.

A handsome man leaned close, whispering words in his ear that he could not hope to understand.

The language was the voice of the fire – transformative and all-consuming.

Everything those words touched would be changed beyond recognition, stripped down to their innermost structure, then warped to his will.

The man was naked, he wore a long leather coat, he was made of fire from his hovering feet to the tips of his wings, his fingers were icy cold, his hands shone like the sun, his eyes absorbed every photon of light, everywhere that man touched him Ronan burned, and burned, and burned.

There were claws around his throat.

There was a hand on his shoulder, shaking him awake.

"Hey! Hey, mister! Come on, wake up!" The voice sounded oddly familiar, and more than a little panicked. "You're projecting, dude, I've got enough of my own pain to deal with! You gotta get it together!"

Who was speaking to him? One of his platoon? No, no one under his command would address him like that.

"It's Major, thank you very much," Ronan murmured thickly between lips gummed with sleep.

"Oh, I don't care, just keep the noise down," the voice huffed. The hand patted apologetically at his shoulder for a moment, then released him. "Do you hear that?"

As he opened his eyes Ronan found himself staring at a mass of straggly black hair hanging inches from his face, and the edge of a striking profile.

He'd thought this man was a dream. Or a hallucination.

This wasn't the man who'd burned him. No. No one had burned him. The thing in the desert had *saved* him. That being was not this man. Half-asleep as he was, Ronan's brain was caught in a loop.

Was this man even real?

The nerves in his shoulder insisted that the hand had been real, and warm.

'The beautiful prick.' The words appeared in his mind as if someone else had thought them for him.

He could feel himself turning red. This was the guy he'd spoken to so inappropriately last time he woke. Which meant that had been real, too.

Ronan wanted to look down at his legs, but the man was still leaning over him, staring intently towards a door that must have been previously hidden by a curtain.

He was in the hospital. He must have passed out. Maybe he'd been shouting in his sleep – perhaps that's what the man had meant about keeping the noise down.

Based on the general gloom it was still night-time, or possibly early morning. Not a normal time to be sociable.

A thin shaft of light came from the partially open door, cutting across the floor to highlight the man's eyes and the edge of his prominent nose. Ronan would have looked towards the door but he found himself transfixed as the nervous tip of a pink tongue dragged across the man's full lips. What a nice view. And so temptingly close.

"Shhhhh," the man hissed, like Ronan had said something out loud. Maybe he had. Again. Whatever medication they had him on, it must be good.

The light vanished for a moment, interrupted by something moving on the other side of the door. There was a snuffling noise.

"Do you believe in werewolves?" the man asked quietly, slowly edging around the bed.

Ah. So this was one of those wake-up-from-a-dream-but-you're-still-dreaming dreams, then?

He wondered if he was ever going to wake up.

Just the same, a dream about werewolves would be more fun than reliving the loss of his legs again. If he couldn't be awake, then staying in this dream would be the next best thing.

"Yes," Ronan said, "of course."

"What? Really?" The figure paused at the end of the bed. "This is usually the point when people call me mad or try to leave."

Ronan shrugged as best he could. "I met a woman once who'd lived as a pub cat for close to a decade. I'm not sure I believe in the influence of the moon, but I can't see any reason *not* to believe in lycanthropy."

"I like you." In the dim light, teeth sparkled in a wide grin. "You're different. I'm Byron, by the way."

"Cox," he replied without thinking. Too many years in the British army.

Byron's grin was pure pornography. "What about cocks? I can show you mine, but now isn't really the time."

Ronan felt his eye twitch.

No.

A werewolf dream might be fun, but he'd had enough of *that* bullshit in basic training.

"You know what?" he said, rolling himself deliberately away from the figure beside the bed. "I don't have to take this kind of abuse from my own subconscious. I don't care if it's wearing a gorgeous face – this isn't real. I'm going back to sleep, or rather, I'm going back to the previous layer of this dream. Sort out your own damn werewolf."

"Wait, what?"

Screwing his eyes shut Ronan forced himself back towards sleep.

He roused twice at the sound of scuffling and the heavy drag of furniture across floor tiles, but his brain was still full of medication, so he soon drifted off again.

Ronan woke this time to brilliant sunshine, shouting, and the sight of what seemed to be a TV cabinet blocking the only exit.

He glanced at the other side of the room. The huge muscular man was asleep across the end of his own bed, long limbs trailing in every direction and blood seeping from under the bandages around his shoulder.

So.

They'd put him in a room with a crazy person.

Fantastic.

Well, he had no wish to wake a lunatic without an escape route, and the window was out of the question. He'd have to sort out this mess himself.

Sitting up, he swung his legs out of bed and – with one hand on the mattress – he tottered three steps towards the door before he realized what he was doing.

He looked down at his legs. The legs he knew he'd lost somewhere over Iraq. They were whole, and definitely his – he recognized the pattern of freckles and the selkie bite scar on his foot from that seaside accident when he was seven.

The white dressings were gone. In their place two long, livid wounds ran down his lower thighs, over his knees and towards his shins, a regimented line of staples holding the skin together.

Finally, the pain hit him like a freight train.

His mysterious legs folded under him as they realized that they couldn't hold his weight.

There wasn't much he could do to stay upright, but he did his best to fall sideways rather than forward to avoid doing any further damage to his legs. Unfortunately, this meant crashing into the other bed on his way down.

For some reason his brain reminded him, on the way to the floor, that last night the man had introduced himself as Byron. Well, it seemed that his name was consistent with his behavior – mad, bad, and dangerous to know.

The man in question sat up with a snort. "Dah fu–"

From his awkward position on the floor Ronan got a fine view of a leggings-wrapped arse and the chart hanging at the bottom of the bed. "Benjamin Williams". So not called Byron, then. Had that just been a dream? He'd had a lot of weird dreams recently.

He shifted his head to stare at the cabinet blocking the door. It certainly looked sturdy enough to keep a werewolf out. Why else would it be across the door? To keep out whoever was currently knocking? Maybe, but why?

Ronan rubbed at his eyes in the vague hope that would make things clearer. It didn't help. All he managed to do was irritate cuts and bruises he hadn't noticed yet.

An upside-down face half-framed by shaggy hair was peering at him from the other side of the bed. The man seemed to have reopened all his wounds – his bandages were soaked, and across his uncovered cheek dried trails of blood showed how his head had been angled while he slept.

Ronan should not have found him attractive in such a terrible state, and yet... His libido had always had terrible timing.

"What are you doing on the floor?" the man asked, more confused than concerned.

In the corridor the shouting had grown louder. "Security! Open up!"

"Oh, you know," Ronan replied with faux nonchalance. "I just fancied a change of scenery. It has absolutely nothing to do with the fact that you barricaded us in here like a lunatic in a zombie movie!"

The man's eyebrows shot up. Or down, since he was still hanging over the bed. One of them had a ring through it. Fresh blood had started to seep from the other one. "You like zombie movies?"

"No! I don't! And that wasn't the relevant part of that statement! Move the fucking cabinet before security kicks the door in!" By the end Ronan knew he was shouting with the voice he usually saved for foolish new recruits, but he wasn't exactly in the best of moods right now.

"Wow, no need to get pissy!" the strange man said, clambering down from the bed, watching his step as he picked his way around Ronan's recumbent form. When his eyes passed over Ronan's legs, he turned pale. "Oh, shit, look at your legs! Fuck! Did you try to get out of bed? Fuck, I am so, so sorry!"

"Yes, fine, you're sorry. Just move that thing, and then help me up," Ronan snapped while probably-Benjamin shambled on towards the door, still trailing apologies. After a moment Ronan remembered his manners. "Please."

"Yeah, yeah, sure. Absolutely."

After a few horrible scraping noises, the cabinet was pushed away, the door was finally opened, and worried medical staff flooded the room.

Two orderlies moved Ronan back to his bed in the end – his roommate was too busy explaining to the rest of the staff that a strange man had tried to break into their room overnight.

Despite his height and his massive shoulders, he somehow contrived to look small as he spoke, sheepishly running the fingers of his left hand through his hair as if he could fix the tangled mess if he just fidgeted enough. His right arm hung limp at his side.

The most senior-looking doctor in the group was not convinced by his story. She seemed to be checking the young man's medical chart. Even at this distance Ronan could see the words 'psychiatric history.'

In an uncharacteristically charitable act, Ronan sat up against the restraining hands of the orderlies and – in his best parade ground tones – said, "He's telling the truth, someone did try to get in here. Several times. Not medical staff either."

"Major Cox, you should be resting!" the doctor admonished, dismissing his actual words with a wave of her hand.

"Resting? How can I rest?" he asked. "I have been given no information as to my current whereabouts. Or my medical status. The last thing I remember clearly is being shot out of the sky in an active war zone, and you think my response to your lax security should be to 'rest'?"

Ronan's eyes were focused on the doctor but he still noticed the relieved smile his roommate gave him.

"But Major..."

"No. Don't you 'But Major' me!" Ronan spat, exhausted and fighting down the pain in his legs. "Go and speak with your security team. And get someone in here to check that man's arm, before he loses the use of it!"

Finally, someone noticed the fact that the other man was bleeding.

The next few hours they each spent dealing with their own problems.

The other man *was* called Byron, though he'd been admitted under his birth name of Ben Williams, apparently by his parents. He insisted that he had changed it legally, and refused to answer to anything else, which only antagonized the staff further.

That argument would probably have raged all day if it hadn't been interrupted by the arrival of a livid surgeon and two physiotherapists – it seemed that Ronan had been correct in his assessment that Byron's function was at risk.

In the relative peace that followed, Ronan finally got the chance to speak to a Ministry of Defence representative who explained exactly how he'd come to be in a private hospital on the wrong continent.

He wasn't in Iraq.

He wasn't even in England.

He was in Washington D.C., in a civilian hospital six thousand miles away from where he was supposed to be.

Very little of this explanation made sense. If Ronan hadn't known better, he'd have thought someone had dosed him with hallucinogens.

The representative spoke about how a mysterious local near the battlefield had sent up a distress flare at precisely the right moment; how his injuries had looked far worse on the ground than they did once he was evacuated; how his troops had managed to escape from the trap that should have slaughtered them all – even the one he was certain had suffered a direct missile hit; and finally how an unnamed friend of his commanding officer had arranged his transfer to the States for specialist surgery.

It was nonsense.

Ronan couldn't help mentally replaying his conversation with the being that had probably been an ifrit.

Over and over he'd told himself that couldn't have been real, that no one could be that lucky, but – against the odds, his platoon had survived. He had his legs. He *knew* he'd lost his legs, he remembered seeing the space where they should have been, he'd seen his boot sitting two meters away and still occupied by his foot.

It *must* have been that creature who had put him back together, however that had been done.

He hoped that the terms of their inadvertent deal were satisfied now. He had freed the creature, and, in turn, it had healed him. They hadn't shared a language, but surely the debt was repaid now.

Ronan really didn't need another blood oath in his life.

Finally, alone in his curtained-off portion of the room, he sighed and stared at the ceiling once more, idly flicking his fingertips along the edges of the physiotherapy guides he'd been given. The road to recovery would be a long one, but he wouldn't start walking down it until tomorrow.

The other half of the room had been quiet for a while. He wondered if his roommate was even in there anymore.

"Major Cock?" a voice whispered, as if Byron had read his mind. "Are you there?"

"Yeah. And it's Cox. With an X. Or you can just call me Ronan."

"Majorly roaming cocks? Roaming where? Across the prairie, a majestic phallic herd..."

The curtain separating their portions of the room pulled back to reveal his tormentor. Neither of them could reach it, but in a fancy hospital like this lots of things would be automated. He didn't like the idea of a privacy screen he didn't have full control over.

Ronan looked at the remote control for his bed and wondered how he could use that to close the curtains again. He couldn't see the button so he fixed Byron with a quelling glare instead.

"I'm in the army, do you really think I haven't heard all those jokes before?"

Byron opened his mouth with an expression like he was going to continue on regardless, but after a moment he turned his eyes away. He looked so downcast Ronan almost felt bad for being annoyed with him.

"Thanks," he mumbled. "For earlier, I mean. I've, uh, had some mental health issues in the past. I didn't tell them what was *really* in the corridor, but they still wouldn't have believed me if you hadn't spoken up."

Ronan shrugged. Poor security was a genuine cause for concern. It would have needed to be addressed eventually, although he would have preferred to do so with a little less drama.

He wasn't going to mention the werewolf issue.

He'd just decided his legs had been returned by a supernatural being, he didn't have any standing to challenge the other man's ideas right now.

Ha, *standing*. He shook his head at his own accidental pun.

The thought of his mysterious recovery reminded him of exactly how badly his lower half was aching. He shifted slightly, already knowing there wasn't a more comfortable position available to him.

"How are your legs?" Byron asked, as if he'd intuited Ronan's thoughts from his movements.

"Killing me." Ronan gave him a smile that he hoped conveyed the idea that he didn't blame Byron from his discomfort. "And you? How's the arm?"

"They don't know if I'll get the full use back," he said in a small voice, left hand tracing over the fingers of his right. "I start physiotherapy tomorrow. It's gonna hurt."

"Me, too. We should be workout buddies," Ronan suggested. He bristled when Byron responded to that statement with a snort. "What?"

"Have you ever been in a gym in your life?"

"I'll have you know I've passed every physical test the army has ever set for me," he snapped back, "I just happen to be built for speed." He glanced down at his legs. "Well, I was."

"You look like you could get blown away by a strong wind!"

"You're exceptionally rude, you know that, right?"

Byron shrugged his uninjured shoulder. "Though I guess with a name like Major Cox you're probably the one doing the blowing." He cackled at his own joke.

"Oh, my sweet summer child, you have no idea," Ronan said, deciding it would be easier to fight fire with fire, as it were.

Byron nearly gave himself whiplash as he turned to stare at him. "Wait, what?"

"Nothing. Nothing at all." Ronan batted innocent golden eyelashes. "Why don't you tell me all about your werewolf theory? Take my mind off my legs?"

Ronan might have thought twice before making that request if he'd had any idea of Byron's unparalleled skill for talking endlessly about his interests. But his deep, earnest voice had charmed him, and letting him talk gave Ronan an excuse to stare at him.

At some point during the interlude Byron's dressings had been changed, and the blood washed away. He was still shirtless – seemingly unable to wear anything over his wounds – and still incredibly muscular. Not that Ronan made a habit of ogling people, but Byron clearly knew that Ronan was looking. He kept flexing his abs.

Sadly, even a gorgeous view and an enthusiastic narrator wasn't enough to keep Ronan awake. He fell asleep somewhere around the fourth hour, in the middle of a monologue on secret government research ships.

That night he dreamt about nuzzling his face against warm abdominal muscles while his hands massaged firm powerful thighs.

He should have felt guilty for fantasizing about a man he'd just met, but after the previous night he was just glad to be dreaming about a normal human being.

3

"URGH." THERE WAS NO DENYING IT, STUBBLE HAD TURNED TO SCRUFF. The disapproving voices of a hundred superior officers echoed in Ronan's ears as he scrubbed at his jaw.

How long had it been since the incident? He'd slept for much of it but he thought probably five days. It had been three days since he woke up to the door barricaded shut. Time zones made things difficult but he was sure his last mission had been two days before that.

What day it was didn't really matter anymore – he'd been discharged from the army. He didn't have anywhere to be.

Leaning close to the mirror, he studied his reflection with a critical eye. He was already well on his way to a full beard.

Despite the bruises and general tiredness, the overall effect wasn't actually that bad. After so many days without shaving he'd expected to look messy and unkempt. Instead he seemed older, but somehow friendlier; the harsh lines of his habitually severe expression hidden behind warm gold-red fuzz.

The last time he'd let his beard grow had been during the worst hangovers of his university days. Back then the hair had been sparse so he'd just looked foolish. Now it was much thicker, and a nice contrast to his sun-bleached strawberry-blond hair and pale skin.

He quite liked this look.

He'd kiss himself.

Perhaps he'd keep it for a while. He didn't need to shave if he didn't want to – regulations didn't apply to him anymore.

That was a depressing thought.

What little happiness he'd found in his new look fluttered out of his grasp.

He was being stupid. He had so much to be thankful for – he'd thought he had lost his legs, losing his career meant nothing in comparison to that – but still, his heart ached.

There was no reasoning with trauma.

His routine had always been important to him. Would it help him feel grounded if he shaved anyway?

He leaned heavily against the sink, trying to keep the weight off his knees, and glanced at his right hand. His fingers were shaking. Whether it was exhaustion, pain, or emotion he couldn't tell – but he knew better than to risk putting a blade near his face in his current state.

Let it grow.

The change might do him some good.

A knock at the door made him jump, air hissing between his teeth as pain blossomed up his legs.

"You ok in there, Major?" Worry was creeping in at the edges of Byron's voice.

The turn took infinite care – shifting his feet inch by inch, one hand gripping the sink so hard that his knuckles paled – until he was finally in a position to open the lock.

Byron was leaning against the door frame, the fingers of his left hand gently flexing the ones on the right, compulsively testing the nerve responses. At the sight of Ronan trembling with effort to stay standing he tried to raise an eyebrow and failed, teeth bared briefly in pain.

"Dude," he drawled, eyes judgmentally flickering over Ronan's form as he stumbled to the waiting wheelchair, "I know they said you should get back on your feet as soon as possible, but I think they meant for you to do that in the therapy sessions. You know, where people can help you if you fall over? Not alone in a tiny bathroom where you could be trapped for hours before someone finds you?"

"In the three days since I woke up you've spent a total of eight hours in front of that mirror." Ronan said sourly, turning the wheelchair towards the door.

The dressings on Byron's face had been removed the day after Ronan woke up. The wounds were a mess of both cuts and burns, but it was the configuration that made people look twice. One deep gash ran down the side of his face, surrounded by thinner perpendicular cuts. Almost as if he'd been hit with a razor-sharp television aerial. Despite the extent of his wounds Byron hadn't stopped his beauty routine. For a man vain enough to top up his eyeliner every day he seemed oddly unbothered by his injuries.

"I doubt I'd have been waiting long for you to rescue me," Ronan continued. "Besides, I needed a piss. It's not my fault they've mysteriously put me in a room with a narcissist and an inaccessible bog."

The door to their shared room ricocheted off the wall as he threw it open with unnecessary force and wheeled himself out into the corridor.

"Wow. Who crapped in your cereal this morning?" Byron sounded just as irritated as he loped along beside the chair.

Ronan tried not to notice the way Byron's muscular thighs moved in his tight black leggings. The fact that the man's backside was at his eye level did not help.

"You've no right to be judging me for overdoing things, when you moved that damn cabinet against the door *again* last night," he snapped. "What the bloody hell are you playing at?"

"It came back. The werewolf."

"What?" Ronan stopped abruptly in the middle of the corridor, the back of his chair digging viciously into Byron's hip as he crashed into him.

"Jesus, Ronan, warn a guy."

"What do you mean 'it came back'?"

"Someone tried the door again."

"And what did you see?"

"Yeah. Something huge – all tall and furry, with clawed hands," Byron said, vaguely gesturing with his left hand to indicate something close to seven feet tall.

With a muttered apology, Ronan dragged Byron forward by the waistband of his leggings, and out of the path of a gaggle of running nurses. This was not the place to be having this kind of conversation.

Glancing around at the other occupants of the corridor, Ronan lowered his voice, hoping his companion would do the same.

"Was it standing upright? Like a person?"

"Yeah, sure."

"Byron, have you ever seen an actual werewolf?" Ronan asked.

When the other man failed to answer beyond a slack-jawed stare, he sighed and began rolling down the corridor again, though this time at a more sensible pace. "We'll talk about this later, okay? Let's just get therapy over with. After that I'm going to try to visit the security office. Then we'll talk."

He'd made it a few yards before he realized Byron wasn't following him. He paused, peering back over his shoulder. "What?"

"Are you saying you *have* seen a real-life werewolf?"

"Like I said, we'll talk about this later." Without medical professionals around, Ronan added, in the privacy of his own head. He didn't want his doctors adding any psychiatric notes to his own medical records.

"Yeah, once they write that shit down, you're pretty much doomed," Byron muttered. He gave a passing medical student a look so dark that the man actually stepped around him and almost walked into the wall.

Inexplicably Byron's expression turned guilty, as if he hadn't meant to frighten the man. At six feet, four inches tall in his bare feet and built like he could lift a car, Byron's base state was vaguely threatening, and that was before the tattoos.

There was probably no way to dress him up to look harmless. Right now, he was wearing an old band shirt with so much of the sides cut away it looked more like a frame for his muscles. Naturally, this also highlighted the stained dressings that ran around his entire shoulder before disappearing down his front.

He looked like he'd be in a fight and no one would want to see the other guy.

That may well have been what happened.

Byron hadn't volunteered any of the details of how he'd been injured, and Ronan hadn't asked for them. So far, they'd just bickered and talked about bullshit.

In a way it was pleasant not to talk about anything serious.

Ronan didn't want to talk about his own injuries. He'd rather focus on other things.

Like this werewolf problem.

It had been a while since he'd last dealt with anything strange. If one didn't count the supernatural entity that gave him his legs back less than a week ago. Ronan couldn't really say he'd 'dealt' with that. If anything, the ifrit had dealt with him.

Regardless, he liked a good mystery.

It was impossible to pinpoint precisely where the strangeness all started. Some things had always been a part of his life.

Imaginary friends. That's what his mother had called them, in that worried but cheerful voice she'd always used when he said anything unusual. His father has dismissed almost anything Ronan had done outside of school or sports as nothing but 'foolish daydreams.'

But Grandpa Edwin? Whenever young Ronan had spoken to him – about the crying girl in the attic; or the terrifying thing in the basement; or the creature that he thought had caused all the collisions on the sharp corner by the village pub? Well, Edwin just laughed and winked. Which wasn't entirely reassuring, but it allowed Ronan to feel heard. His grandfather always seemed to know more than he was willing to say, and even as a small child he'd soon learned to read between the lines.

If his grandfather wasn't concerned then Ronan probably shouldn't be either. So, for years he'd tried not to worry about what he saw, no matter how scary things might be.

Ronan first encountered the creature that changed that on Beltane, 1989, in an isolated part of the woodland that took up half his grandfather's run-down estate. He'd been eight at the time, and he had never forgotten that first sighting, as innocuous as it had been.

A fast-flowing stream began in a deep gully that had once been an open mine, centuries earlier.

Some former owner of the land had seen fit to build a folly around it, to capture the water in an artificial pool. But the sides of the basin had cracked over time, and the columns had fallen into moss-covered ruin.

Ronan had loved that place. The soft green light and the gentle bubbling of water. It was quiet and peaceful, not like the bustle of school, or the odd atmosphere of the house with all its whispers and screams that no one else could hear.

The stream was a lovely place. It had not needed the addition of pan flute music. Nothing in the universe needed the addition of pan flute music, certainly not from a shirtless man with alarmingly furry legs.

Thankfully, the man wasn't real. Ronan had an active imagination, and had just watched too many fanciful television shows over the Christmas break. That was where the faun had come from. This being, who sat and stared and never, ever approached him, was just another 'imaginary friend' like the others. He was no more real than Santa Claus and could be safely ignored. Just like all the others.

So, Ronan had ignored him, as much as he could in the circumstances.

Just because you're ignoring someone, that doesn't make them not exist. He was still there, loitering in the shadows. As Ronan aged, he became increasingly uncomfortable with the creature's presence. Something about the faun started to feel vaguely threatening and improper. But he couldn't put his finger on it, so he let it be.

Finally, at fourteen, Ronan attended an assembly at school about sexual harassment and that one nagging detail finally clicked into place. Fauns are very beautiful. Fauns don't wear trousers. Fauns are very well endowed. They really *should* wear trousers.

Although this particular individual had made no moves on him whatsoever, young Ronan had been very certain that naked mythological creatures should not be hanging around teenage boys. The creature had to go.

That evening he drove the faun out of the grove with what had been – on reflection from half a lifetime away – a rather embarrassing cocktail of holy water, garlic, and silver shavings. Anyone with an ounce of sense would have run away from a screaming teenager throwing smelly water balloons at them.

If an older, wiser, and legally adult Ronan – one who'd, by then, travelled far and wide and engaged in sexual acts with more supernatural species than most people have ever heard of – returned to the grove to apologize to the faun in person a decade later, well, who could blame him?

After all, the creature was very beautiful. And very well endowed.

Despite his injuries, Byron was still a very attractive man. One whose leggings left nothing to the imagination. No wonder Ronan kept thinking about that faun.

They were outside for the first time since Ronan had woken up. He'd forgotten what cool breezes felt like without all the layers of his combat uniform in the way. He would have liked to enjoy the fresh air too, but instead he had to settle for summer city smog under the clove scent of Byron's black cigarette.

"What do you mean 'it's not a werewolf'?" Byron asked as he paced up and down, smoking in the secretive way of someone who still expected to get caught by their mother. "I saw it, man! It was seven feet tall! It had claws! It tried to get in and eat us while we slept! How is that not a werewolf?"

Ronan didn't really understand his agitation.

It was a warm, sunny day in June. Birds were singing, flowers were blooming, somewhere in the distance a radio was playing at an antisocial volume, and a woman in pink scrubs had just walked face first into a lamppost because she'd been too busy staring at Byron's chest. Ronan really couldn't blame her – it was an excellent view. He'd abandoned his shirt half way through the therapy session, claiming that even cut down it was too heavy on his shoulder.

They were alive. Life was good.

"You can't say it was going to eat us in our sleep," Ronan tried to reason. He was lounging in his wheelchair, aching legs stretched out in front of him and chin resting on one fist, pretending not to stare at his roommate as he walked up and down.

"What else do werewolves do?"

"Not a werewolf. I've seen the security footage." That had been something of an achievement on its own – he was clearly a patient and had no right to access that kind of information. He'd learned long ago that getting most things in life was a matter of attitude, and the right tone of voice.

They would never have shown it to Byron. He looked far too unusual to be trustworthy.

"Werewolf means a man that turns into a wolf," Ronan went on while Byron continued his sullen pacing. "That thing was a seven-foot biped, not a gigantic wolf or a dog standing on its hind legs. It moved with a human gait. Even if some dogs can stand like that, they can't walk like us, their skeletal structure is all wrong. It might have had claws but they were attached to hands, not paws. Therefore, not a werewolf. I mean, there's no evidence on the video that it changes form at all. There's a chance it isn't a were-anything."

"Then how the fuck did it get into the hospital looking like that?" Byron asked with a pointed finger, as if he'd found the flaw in Ronan's argument.

Ronan shrugged, leaning back in his chair and trying to pretend that he wasn't enjoying the scent of clove smoke and cologne that Byron's gesture had sent his way. "An open window? Service tunnels? The sewage system? I dunno, there are lots of options."

"I don't really care *what* it is. I just want it to stay out of our room." Byron said in what felt like a lie. He was curious, Ronan could tell. He'd often felt that way himself when he ran into something he didn't recognize. "Come on then, Major, use your military training, what do we do?"

Ronan's first instinct was to tell him to leave it alone. He didn't like getting into someone else's business, but it *had* tried to get into their room, which made the creature's behavior their business, too.

Feeling terribly British, he suggested, "We could start by asking what it wants?"

"So, that went well!" Byron shouted as he ran half-crouching down the dimly lit service tunnel somewhere under the hospital, pushing Ronan ahead of him as the great shambling beast fought to fit through the narrow cable-strewn space behind him.

"Shut up and hang a left!"

"I'm just saying, 'ask it what it wants' might be the best plan I've ever heard! It's up there with such greats as 'getting involved in a land war in Asia' and 'no, Mr Bond, I expect you to die'. It's genius..."

"The other bloody left!" Ronan bellowed over Byron's continued complaints. "For fuck's sake, shut up and run!"

The creature had shown up at their door almost as soon as lights out had been called that night. They'd planned to sit up and wait for it, a supply of cold cafeteria coffee and energy drinks on hand to get them through the long hours that never came. Instead Byron had almost choked on his first sip when he heard the sound of claws on the door handle.

Throwing an almost full can of sugary caffeine directly at the thing's head had not been part of the plan, but it had been effective at driving the monster back. It didn't seem to be expecting any kind of resistance, and fled when Byron followed his first throw with a less expertly tossed chair.

They'd followed the giant dog-faced thing through the hospital as best they could – Ronan forced to split off to take the elevator down while Byron thundered after the thing like a man possessed – down into the basement level.

Something about the chase had highlighted the perfection of Byron's form. In a ridiculously romantic moment, Ronan had thought that he looked like a mythic hero hidden under a veneer of fashion – someone destined to vanquish the monster with ease.

But luck and destiny had not been on their side. By the time they'd regrouped, the trail had gone cold. The hospital campus was a vast, sprawling space filled with strange noises and obscure hiding places.

When they'd finally cornered the thing – in a service closet near the medical waste furnaces – at half past five in the morning, they were exhausted. So exhausted that they didn't immediately realize that they were in an enclosed space with an unknown creature, no conventional weapons, and no one knew where they were.

Still, Ronan had pressed on with the plan.

Even though he'd asked with perfect politeness, they never did receive an answer to the question 'what do you want?'

Byron had almost received a face full of claws and rage before they ran, which was a kind of answer.

The thing was angry.

Why it was angry didn't really matter when it seemed intent on eviscerating them.

More importantly – they were lost.

Although Ronan had paid careful attention to their route through the tunnels, it was difficult to navigate while being pushed by someone who insisted on complaining loudly the whole time.

As they turned down one of the better-lit corridors, he was horrified to see a door swing open and an elderly janitor peer out. Ronan was struck by a sudden impression of being in a children's cartoon when the man, instead of ducking back to his room and closing the door, began to run after them. Now there was a screaming old man between them and the monster.

How could this possibly get any worse? He tried not to think about that question too much – he knew full well that things could always get worse.

"What the fuck do we do?" Byron shouted.

For an instant Ronan noticed a faint beam of light above their heads as they turned a corner. Not the sort of light that comes from a bulb. It might not help but they didn't have any other options.

"Outside!" Getting his phone from his pocket took much longer than it should have, but he finally fumbled it free and held down the button for the voice assistant. "What time will sunrise be?"

"Sunrise was at 5:42 today," replied the vaguely mechanical voice.

He twisted in his chair to speak to the janitor running breathlessly behind them. Byron's torso was so wide he had to lean out further than he would have liked. The chair tipped slightly but Byron kept them moving.

"What's the shortest route outside?" he shouted, then yelped when Byron pushed him back into his seat. A large circuit box whizzed by, right where his head would have been.

"Two rights and a left, there's a fire door!" came the wheezing response.

"Did you get that or do you need help with directions again?" Ronan joked up at Byron, too full of adrenaline to worry about the situation.

"Just point where you want me to go!" Byron growled under his breath. He didn't look like he was having fun. Maybe this wasn't the time for humor.

The light of dawn was blinding as they burst through the double doors, Ronan leaning forward to hit the crash bar and protect his knees from any ricochet. In one surprisingly smooth motion, Byron swung the chair out of the way, grabbed the janitor by a hand and shoved him in the same direction.

He had only a moment to step back into the path of the oncoming beast.

As the creature swarmed out of the doorway into the light, Byron squared up and delivered a devastating left hook to where its head should have been.

He missed.

A bearded middle-aged man stood there instead, naked and blinking in the rays of the sun.

Moving on instinct Byron adjusted his aim and punched him in the face instead. The man dropped like a stone.

"What the fuck?" he muttered, poking at the body with a toe. When it didn't respond he crouched down to roll it over. "Uncle Mac?"

4

HOW EXACTLY DOES ONE EXPLAIN SUCH STRANGE CIRCUMSTANCES TO security? Why you were being pushed in a wheelchair through restricted areas of a hospital, by a shirtless fellow patient, while being pursued by a naked friend of that patient's family? Or why that friend is now unconscious?

With confidence, dignity, a straight face, and more bullshit than an Australian cattle station.

"Oh my god, oh my fucking GOD, I can't believe you got away with that!" Byron giggled as he slammed the door to their room shut behind them. A man that size should not be giggling but Ronan would be damned if it wasn't the most adorable sound he'd ever heard.

"I can't believe you tried to have a one-armed fist fight with a giant monster!" Ronan laughed, hauling himself out of the chair and tottering awkwardly in the direction of his bed.

He'd been looking forward to standing up after so many hours in the cold basement, but now he realized the chill had stiffened his joints more than he had expected. And the bed was suddenly so very far away.

Before he could complain, Byron squeezed an undignified squeak out of him by grabbing him and lifting him up against his chest as if he weighed nothing at all.

"Holy fuck, you're strong!" Ronan gasped, then laughed again.

Byron grinned up at him, adjusting the position of his arm under Ronan's arse to keep a better grip on him. Ronan wasn't a heavy man but he'd never been held like that before. His heart was doing some very strange things.

"That was amazing." Byron said.

"It was stupid."

"It was wild!"

"Idiotic!"

"It was hot." Byron's tone shifted deeper, his eyes darkening.

Ronan licked his lips. "So fucking hot."

Somehow the kiss took them both by surprise.

Byron gasped against Ronan's lips, his injured right arm coming up to wrap carefully around Ronan's back, not for stability but seemingly out of a need to be as close as possible.

Following his lead, Ronan sank his fingers into artfully messy hair, the pad of his right thumb brushing across the fuzz of Byron's side shave.

He'd never been inclined towards extravagant fashion – after years of army haircuts he should have found the style ridiculous. Instead, he quickly found himself fascinated by the texture of long curls and stubble side-by-side.

In a way that seemed to sum up what Byron was – a collection of contrasts that should not have worked so well together. Muscles and eyeliner, tattoos and scars, deep voice and an infectious grin, horrible taste in music and a mouth that would get him into trouble one day, and that face, those eyes, those lips.

None of that should have appealed to Ronan. His taste in humans had always run towards the tweedy sort who looked like they graduated from Oxbridge and owned horses. But perhaps that was the point. Ronan rarely dated humans. He'd always had varied tastes when it came to the more mysterious creatures lurking in the hidden corners of the world.

His thoughts were interrupted by the touch of cool fabric against the back of his thighs. Byron had carried them across the room so smoothly Ronan hadn't noticed they were moving until they bumped into the bed. He'd been too distracted with thinking, and by the soft warmth of lips.

"Sorry," Byron rumbled. The sound turned into a gasp of pain when he tried to follow the kiss with an affectionate nuzzle that disturbed the half-healed burn across his face. He leaned back enough to give Ronan a rueful smile.

"Guess I'm not as healed as I thought," he said. As if to highlight that his right hand was clearly trembling as it drifted down to stroke the crease at the top of Ronan's thighs. "I really want to fuck you right now, but I suppose we can't."

"Humph," Ronan muttered noncommittally. He had half a mind to take him up on the offer, knees and shoulders be damned, but he was thirty-five. He knew better than to risk both their recoveries for half an hour of pleasure. Still, they weren't complete invalids.

"I figured with all that ink you'd be a more imaginative soul than that," he said, raising a challenging eyebrow.

Certain that he had Byron's attention, he bent to kiss the uninjured side of his neck, shifting after a few soft kisses to drawing complex patterns on his skin with his tongue. Just when Byron shivered, he ended the contact by sucking a bruise over his clavicle. No one would notice another mark amongst the others.

"Do you remember I said I'd heard all the nicknames before?" Ronan winked. "I promise you I've earned every one of them."

Byron's smile widened to a grin. "Oh, well, now I'm intrigued. Tell me more."

"I'd much rather show you."

"You absolutely earned every single pornographic nickname that anyone has ever given you," Byron mumbled indistinctly.

Ronan smiled quietly at the ceiling while he stretched and rubbed his throat. Beside him Byron was breathing heavily against his shoulder. The bed should have been too narrow for a pair of grown men – especially given Byron's broad chest and arms – but right now the weight of him was still pleasant.

In fact, everything about him was perfect, as Ronan had just discovered. He'd been entirely right about Byron's proportions; the movement of his muscles under Ronan's hands had been a delight; even the sweat from their ridiculous adventure had tasted sweet.

There was nothing Ronan would have changed.

Except possibly that one tattoo.

As Byron lay naked and face down on the bed Ronan finally had a chance to admire more of his ink. There was a lot of text, though it was impossible to read upside down. A stylized spaceship on one thigh; an angel and a demon falling together down the side of his back; a band logo on his wrist; what looked like a tapir in Elizabethan clothing on his calf – all of those were fine. They were weird, but they were fine.

What was bothering Ronan was the thing on the left side of his stomach. He'd kept on making eye contact with the ugly creature. It was enough to put a man off his rhythm. It hadn't helped that he couldn't work out what it was meant to be, or why it was holding a wrench.

"It's a gremlin," Byron said. "They take apart planes. I used to hang out on airfields a lot when I was a kid, old mechanics like to tell horror stories."

Ronan was already nodding before he realized he hadn't actually asked the question out loud.

"What the fuck?" he asked, his voice crackling a little from the strain on his throat. He should have warmed up more.

"What?" Byron finally lifted his head again. His face was still a little flushed and his already messy hair clung to the sweat on his brow. Somehow, he looked even hotter like this.

Ronan was almost tempted to kiss him. Instead he slapped his arm just below the bandages still covering his bicep.

"Ow. What was that for?"

"I didn't ask you a question."

An odd mixture of expressions danced across Byron's face, confusion warring with tiredness as he tried to work out what Ronan meant.

"You just answered a question that I'd only thought," Ronan said slowly.

In a miracle of cardiovascular recovery Byron blushed from his ears all the way down his chest. From this angle Ronan would have sworn that even his arse turned pink.

Byron opened his mouth, seemed to think better of it, and looked away instead of speaking.

"Are you spying on me with your mind?" Ronan asked, as carefully as he could, "or are you just picking up on random thoughts like an untuned radio? The first time I woke, you let me think I'd propositioned you when I was out of my mind on opiates. That wasn't very nice."

The tangled mess of Byron's hair was covering most of his face, but Ronan could see that he was biting his lip.

"I'm not spying on you," Byron whispered, "I'm not trying to hear anyone most of the time. Some people are louder than others, and you can be very loud. It can be hard not to overhear things, especially when there's strong emotion behind it."

Ronan wasn't entirely sure that 'I find your tattoo disconcerting' could really be considered a thought with strong emotion, but he wasn't going to argue when he knew almost nothing about the concept.

There were a thousand and one questions he should be asking.

He yawned instead.

"Can you choose to hear my thoughts?"

Byron had shifted his head just enough to look at him through a gap in his hair. He looked almost like a frightened beagle puppy peeking out from behind its ears.

"If I concentrate, I can listen to you when I want to – it's easier to tune in than to entirely tune out – but I don't want to eavesdrop on your thoughts twenty-four seven, Ronan, your mind is your own."

Ronan studied him for a long moment before carefully reaching out to brush away the curtain of hair. Fear, worry, nerves, a touch of guilt. He saw nothing on Byron's face that would make him concerned for his privacy.

Leaning up in bed he pressed a kiss to the bridge of Byron's aquiline nose, careful to avoid the worst of his still healing injuries.

"Okay."

"Okay?"

Byron had closed his eyes as if he didn't quite believe the answer.

"Yeah. We can talk more about this later if you want, but we're okay." The assertion of Ronan's statement was ruined by another yawn. "Sorry, I'm wiped out. I'm guessing you are too, now the adrenaline has worn off. You can stay here if you want, but you have to put some clothes on; it's only midday, I'm amazed no one has walked in on us."

The smile returning to Byron's face felt almost like the sun appearing from behind an especially heavy storm cloud. Ronan couldn't help smiling back.

"Don't worry, no one would have come in," Byron said as he rolled awkwardly off the narrow bed. "I wedged the door closed."

"What? When?" With equally stiff movements Ronan sat up to look. "Huh."

There was in fact a folded magazine jammed under the door.

He turned back to Byron. "Two questions – one, when did you do that? And two, why did you move that entire cabinet like a lunatic the first time you blocked the door?"

Byron was staring at him with the expression of a kid who didn't want to get into more trouble.

"That was just to stop the nurses coming in. A magazine isn't gonna stop a monster, is it?"

It was hard to resist the urge to rub his brow in frustration, so Ronan didn't bother to resist. "I haven't seen you bend down, or move towards the door since we came in here. Care to answer the first question?"

The silent eye contact that followed seemed to drag on forever until it was broken by a movement at the edge of Ronan's vision. Byron's leggings were rising off the floor on the opposite of the bed to where their owner was standing.

Ronan pinched the bridge of his nose. "Telekinesis? Seriously?"

"I can only lift a few pounds."

"Oh, yeah, because everyone can lift a couple of kilos *with their mind*, that's perfectly normal! Look, I'm not mad, I'm just..." Ronan sighed heavily in an attempt to calm down before he went on because he could see Byron's face darkening again. "Did you float a coffee pot in here at five in the morning?"

"Yeah."

"I thought I was fucking hallucinating. I don't know what medications you're on, but that's not a good side effect for mine. Next time, warn a guy. I cut back on my dose when I didn't need to."

"You wouldn't have believed me," Byron snapped. He'd grabbed his leggings as soon as they were close to his hand, and was trying to pull them on but hadn't yet realized that he was trying to get both legs into the same hole. Given that he wasn't wearing underwear it wasn't the most dignified sight.

"I believed you about the 'werewolf' in the end, and I went into the basement with you – I would have believed you about this," Ronan said.

On the last word he had to lean forward to grab Byron's arm to keep him from falling over in his tangled leggings. The unexpected physical contact made Byron look at him again.

"I promise I'll always give you the benefit of the doubt no matter how unbelievable a claim might be." Always was a long time, but Ronan knew he meant what he was saying. "Come on, unblock the door and come back to bed. We need to get some sleep."

For a moment it seemed like Byron would refuse, but finally he nodded.

The bed seemed even more narrow now that the afterglow had truly faded away.

Ronan couldn't complain though. Byron was curled against his side, his injured right arm slung over Ronan's waist and his legs carefully tucked back to keep them from touching Ronan's knees. It was comforting in a way Ronan hadn't felt for months, if not years. Sharing a bed wasn't usually his style.

He closed his eyes, intending to sleep, but after a few breaths he felt Byron's nose nudge against his cheek. His stubble rasped a little as Byron shifted up to press a kiss to his jaw line. Half asleep, he hadn't noticed that Byron's hand had moved down just enough to press his forearm against the front of Ronan's shorts.

"You didn't get off," Byron murmured. "Here, let me help you."

"No. Don't," Ronan said, aiming for a gentle tone but mostly sounding tired.

He felt rather than saw Byron's frown. His hand was moving back.

"It's only fair. I thought you..."

"Hey, shush." Ronan quickly reached down to catch Byron's wrist. Careful not to jar the other man's shoulder, he brought Byron's hand up to his mouth to kiss his palm. He tried to give a reassuring smile when he continued. "As much as I want to experience hands this impressive – and I really, *really* do – I'm full of morphine. It'd be an exercise in futility."

"Are you sure? Not to blow my own horn or anything – because clearly that should be your job from now on – but I'm pretty good at this." Byron laughed.

The warmth of his breath against Ronan's cheek was a wonderful feeling, but he knew his own body too well.

"I've been on these meds before," he said. "It doesn't matter how good you are, you're just going to have to wait for next time. Now, let me sleep."

Sadly, some things were easier said than done.

Almost as soon as his bedmate began to snore, Ronan's mind started to wander. Knowing that his thoughts might be overheard, he'd been trying not to think too much about the two of them. Now that he was technically alone, he couldn't stop his thoughts heading in that direction.

On the face of things, it was ridiculous to have become attached to this strange man so quickly. A few days sharing a hospital room, both seriously injured, lives turned upside down, and their blood no doubt filled with a cocktail of drugs. It was a dangerous mix. Still, they had probably saved a man's life tonight, maybe even two – Mac could easily have been shot if security had caught him down there.

Even though he wasn't Ronan's usual type, Byron was gorgeous in a weird kind of way. They'd moved together with such ease, despite their limitations – in bed as well as during the chase. He felt so good under Ronan's hands.

They'd both made promises of the future without even a second thought – 'from now on', 'next time', 'always.' Ronan didn't know if they had an 'always' ahead of them. He still didn't entirely understand why he was in this particular hospital, or why it wasn't a problem for him to stay. Did he even want to stay?

Whatever Ronan's life was going to look like now, the British Army wasn't going to be an active part of it. What else did he have in his life but that? What else could he have?

Why not this bizarre creature snuffling against his cheek? Why shouldn't he have that?

"No! Don't go into the summer house!"

The scream jerked Ronan awake, his mind instantly on high alert as the mountain of a man beside him sat bolt upright, shaking, one hand outstretched as if to halt someone who wasn't there.

"Hey," Ronan murmured as calmly as he could.

When Byron didn't look back, or give any indication that he was awake, Ronan gently placed a hand at the base of his spine. His fingers covered a tattoo that seemed to be written in Icelandic. He wondered what the words meant. It seemed like every time he looked at Byron's skin, he found something new.

With a deep shuddering breath Byron turned to stare at him, eyes dark and unfocused. If Ronan had been any other man his expression would probably have been terrifying, he looked so unlike himself.

"Byron?" Ronan tried again. "Are you okay?"

He snapped out of it as abruptly as he'd sat up, the haunted look melting away as he pushed back to sit against the headboard. Every part of his body seemed to be trembling.

"Talk with me," Byron said. His voice was rough with sleep or possibly emotion. It was hard to tell as he turned his face towards the ceiling. "I don't care what about, just keep me awake."

"Okay, I can do that," Ronan nodded.

Almost immediately he realized that was a lie, and for a moment he busied himself with joining Byron in sitting comfortably while he tried to think of something to say.

In an effort to keep up the comfort of physical contact, Ronan found himself tracing a fingertip along the bandages around Byron's right shoulder. Why was his mind always blank at times like this?

As he watched his finger following the path of Byron's burns, he found some inspiration.

"You know what happened to me," he said with a gesture towards his knees, "but how did you end up in here?"

A huge hand enveloped his own, carefully lifting it away from the tender skin. When he tilted his head back down Byron had an odd look on his face, a bizarre combination of embarrassment and pride, like he'd done something supremely stupid.

"Have you ever seen a movie stunt and thought, 'wow, I wonder if that's actually possible'?" he asked.

Ah.

So, Byron *had* done something supremely stupid then.

"Well, yes," Ronan reluctantly replied. He already knew this discussion was going to make him cringe, but now he'd raised the topic he couldn't exactly shut it down again. "It's the nature of special effects to be fascinating. Personally, when it comes to copying impressive things from movies, I prefer to learn how to do them through accredited channels – like jumping out of a plane from a few thousand feet. I can't say I've ever tried to work out something like that on my own, but I suppose you did?"

"I wasn't alone."

Ronan sighed. "I know I'm going to regret asking, but – what did you do?"

"Have you heard of the idea of a flaming sword?"

"It's a fairly common mythological concept, off the top of my head I can think of three–"

Byron was grinning at him, the expression somehow highlighting the burns that covered about half his face, and the strange pattern of cuts that had just missed his eye.

"Oh. No. You didn't..." In the face of such reckless stupidity Ronan found it hard to string together an adequate sentence to express his incredulity. "Why would you... Wait, how did a sword make those kinds of marks on your face? How many times did you get cut with it?"

"You wrap a sword in fabric for fuel, then wrap that with wire. To keep the fuel attached." Byron raised a hand towards his cheek but didn't touch his skin. He gestured down towards his shoulder. "The big line is from the sword, the lines coming off that are from the wire. It was very hot."

"What possessed you to–"

"My cousin Darcey is studying for a Masters in physical metallurgy," Byron said, as if this explained everything.

"And that led them to, what, make you a fiery sword? It's not the Middle Ages, you don't–"

"Oh, no, it was fair, she made swords for both of us. It's not a duel if only one person has a sword."

There was no sane response to that.

Telepathy, telekinesis – fine. He could deal with that.

By contrast the words that had just come out of Byron's mouth were triggering every 'commanding officer dealing with an idiot' instinct Ronan had ever developed. It was so stupid that he wanted to get out of the bed just so he could pace up and down while he gave him the rollocking he so richly deserved. Byron was lucky that Ronan's legs were still half asleep.

"Duel?" he asked, fully aware that his tone was dripping with irritation.

Byron didn't seem to notice. "Well, of course, one person with a burning sword is always going to win against anyone with a normal sword. We don't see each other very often, but we were having a drink and she raised the question of what would happen in a fight if both fighters had a flaming blade."

"So, this whole situation was a drunken–"

"Oh no! She'd never try to make something like that when she was drunk." Byron looked truly offended that Ronan would ever make that assumption. "It was the next day. We were completely sober."

"Are you sure? Because you seem to be telling me that you had a duel, with swords, which were on fire. That's not a sober thing to do. How did you not think that was dangerous?"

Byron rolled his eyes and scoffed.

"We've both taken martial arts classes since we were toddlers," he said, "we know how to handle swords."

Ronan wanted to throttle him.

"Byron, full offence, the fact that you're sitting here, in hospital, recovering from major surgery, sort of suggests that at least one of you doesn't know how to handle a red-hot sword! What the actual fuck?"

"It would have been fine if her damn dog hadn't attacked me," Byron huffed, going from offended for his cousin to offended for himself.

As annoyed as Ronan was right now, he couldn't help but notice that when Byron folded his arms the movement was much more balanced than it would have been a few days ago. A clear sign that Byron was healing well.

Ronan tried to hold onto the pleasure he felt at Byron improving and let go of his irritation over the stupidity of the situation. Besides, if there was more to this, he should probably hear him out.

"A dog did this?"

"Yeah, a dumbass fuzzy little mongrel that thinks it's a war dog," Byron said, gesturing with one hand to give the idea of a Pomeranian-sized dog. "Turns out it was rehomed because the kids at its last house liked to play at dragon slaying and hit it a few times. So, it saw us sparring in the backyard and snapped. Knocked me down onto my sword," he touched his jaw, fingers shaking at the memory, "then Darcey fell on me with hers. She's only tiny compared to me, and the sword wasn't even that sharp, but was still a sword. Momentum did the rest. I didn't even realize it had gone through my shoulder – I just thought I'd lost my eye before I passed out. All because of a damn dog. I guess it didn't mean it, though."

Eyebrows raised in disbelief, Ronan stared open-mouthed at Byron's bizarre assessment of the situation.

"You can't exactly say that this wasn't a stunt that was likely to go wrong, I mean, why didn't you use something like iron bars rather than, you know, *actual live swords*? If you weren't actually intending to stab each other."

When Byron finally turned to look at him again, he was wearing an expression that strongly implied that the option had never occurred to him. He looked both horrified and devastated. Maybe Ronan had been too hard on him.

'Well, it's a good thing he's gorgeous,' Ronan thought, running one hand soothingly over a thick tattooed bicep, 'because he's dumb as a brick.'

"Hey!!"

'Oh. Right. The mind reading. Let me apologize,' he thought as he slid his hand down to Byron's hip instead and urged him closer.

"Again? Seriously?" Byron smirked, eagerly twisting around to steal a kiss. "I've known you less than a week, General Deepthroat, and you're already trying to kill me."

Accepting the kiss with enthusiasm Ronan murmured against his lips, "It's Major Cox, thank you."

"Oh, no, I figured you deserve a promotion."

Ronan laughed, and began to wrap his arms around Byron's chest, only to be interrupted by the arrival of dinner and a very surprised-looking member of staff.

"There are two beds in this room for a reason, you know!"

5

"PLEASE, DON'T TELL YOUR DAD ABOUT THIS," THEIR VISITOR SAID, more to his shoes than to Byron.

It was the next day, and Ronan was feeling very out of sorts.

They'd spent a whole night chasing a monster, had managed to talk their way out of getting in trouble for that, had enjoyed a satisfying sexual encounter, slept through most of the day, been caught in bed together by a nurse, and then had another poor night's sleep.

Ronan had assumed that the bad night was caused by disrupting their normal sleep cycle, but he'd drifted off almost as soon as Byron crawled back into bed with him. Now they were sitting separately again, and he had to admit that he felt a little lonely on his own. Byron was ten whole feet away. He was being ridiculous.

"Why would he tell his father?" he asked, in an effort to keep his mind on the topic at hand.

The man Byron had referred to as 'Uncle Mac' looked up guiltily but didn't answer. One of his eyes was swollen shut, and he was still wearing the patient wristband from the emergency room.

Between them they'd managed to pass the whole incident off as a family friend suffering an adverse reaction to seasonal allergy medication, and an unrelated pack of stray dogs hiding in the basement.

The story was pure bullshit.

Anyone with an ounce of sense could have seen that, but, as Ronan had discovered at an early age, most human beings locked their common sense in a cupboard the instant they were faced with anything unusual. No one wanted to look too deeply into the circumstances of a naked man who had done no damage and tested negative for narcotics.

Byron sighed melodramatically and rolled his eyes. Ronan wondered if he'd reapplied his eyeliner that morning just to make the expression even more obnoxious.

"What do you think I'm gonna tell David – 'watch out, Uncle Mac's a werewolf'?"

"Therianthrope," Ronan corrected absently. He'd found a blank notepad in the drawer by his bed, and was making careful notes about the figure in front of him. It had almost been a compulsion when he was younger, to catalogue everything he learned about the 'imaginary friends' he encountered. Like he was some kind of amateur anthropologist. He hadn't really felt the need over the last few years, but Mac was too fascinating not to make notes on.

Just over five feet tall, bearded, and balding, Byron's 'uncle' dressed like an accountant who wanted to be a lumberjack. He certainly didn't look like the kind of guy who turned into a giant monster, nor did he seem the sort to be involved in things like spying.

"Therianthrope, lycanthrope, misanthrope, whatever," Byron snapped. "If I told David about any of that werewolf stuff he'd have me tested again. Or locked up. Why would I risk that?"

"I didn't mean that part," Mac said, still speaking to the toes of his shoes, "though I would appreciate the discretion. I meant – please don't tell your father you saw me. I'm supposed to be undercover. If your mom found out your dad was having me spy on you...you know how she can get, Ben, please. She scares the shit out of me."

"Byron." They corrected him as a chorus, and Ronan couldn't help the way his heart warmed when Byron gave him a grateful smile.

"Sorry," Mac nodded with a grimace, "sorry, Byron, I forgot. Please, don't tell anyone you saw me, please?"

"What I don't understand," Ronan said, circling something in his notes, "is why you would take on a job at a time when you can't keep your form stable? That's incredibly risky."

"I..." The man rubbed his head, clearly uncomfortable. His feet started to shuffle him towards the door, apparently of their own volition. "I don't know why I change. It's not to do with the moon or anything, it just happens. Look, I don't wanna talk about this and the longer I stay in here the more likely I am to be seen. I won't come back, I'll just make up reports for your dad, okay, Byron? Don't do anything rash and no one needs to know, okay?"

Ronan turned to Byron and raised an eyebrow. It was up to Byron whether they said anything or not – technically none of this was Ronan's business.

Byron shrugged his left shoulder. "Fine, sure, I won't mention this to David."

Uncle Mac was out the door before Byron had even finished the sentence.

"So...what do we do now?" Byron asked once they were alone.

Ronan looked up from his notes, confused by the question.

"What do you mean? Neither of us is getting discharged anytime soon, so our options are pretty limited. It's not like we can go downstairs and hunt down the spooky cafeteria ghost or something."

"What?" Now Byron looked confused too. "I meant do you want to watch TV, or go for a walk, or have some sex..."

He winked.

"It's ten in the morning."

"Didn't stop you the other day."

Ronan shoved his notebook onto the shelf beside his bed. "That was mostly adrenaline-fuelled. I'm not sure I'd trust a magazine to keep the door shut again, and I doubt the staff would appreciate walking in on us. Maybe later, when people are less likely to wander in."

"I might hold you to that," Byron said with a grin that turned thoughtful. "There has to be a perfect time, you know, when there's no one walking around."

"When was Mac trying to get in the first two times? No one noticed him then."

The full body shiver of disgust Byron gave in response to that was enough to make Ronan laugh.

"Please don't put the thought of sex and my uncle into my head at the same time, some things shouldn't mix." Byron had been sitting on the edge of his bed ever since Mac came into the room, but now he stood and stretched, shaking out his arms as if to dismiss the entire concept.

He wandered around, touching random objects. He looked like a caged animal. Ronan wondered how bored he must be – with a figure like his he must have spent a lot of time working out. Resting probably wasn't his forte.

"He isn't really your uncle, is he?" Ronan asked, more out of a desire to distract than to know the answer. He vaguely remembered Byron saying something to that effect while security was moving Mac to the emergency room, but he'd been too busy talking to the janitor to pay attention.

"No, he was a friend of David's – my father – when they were younger," Byron explained sadly. "Best friends, really. When I was a kid, any time David was home, Mac was with him. They, uh, they worked together and travelled a lot. Even after David went into business with my actual uncle, he'd still take off all the time. Gianna hated it, and I guess eventually she blamed Mac instead of him."

"Gianna?"

"My mother."

Either the window frame was the most fascinating thing in the world, or Byron was deliberately not making eye contact.

"Ah," Ronan said, as diplomatically as he could. In his experience families were always a mess. In a way he'd been blessed by not having to spend much time around his own.

"We don't get along."

"I figured that from the name thing."

Byron nodded. His fingertips drummed out a beat on the window for a moment or two longer and then stopped when he appeared to reach a decision. "Hey, do you want to go outside? You could wheel downstairs and we could walk slow laps of the garden. Your therapist did say you should be walking more with the crutches. Obviously, I could always keep an arm around your waist, you know, to hold you up."

"Not so you can grope my arse whenever you feel like it, then?"

"Oh, no, absolutely not."

Byron lied.

"Do you want to tell me how you ended up named after a famous mad poet?" Ronan asked on their second slow turn around the grounds. The hospital had done its best to make the space welcoming, but it was boring as all hell, and Ronan suspected he was going to go mad if the silence dragged out much longer.

"There's a poet called Byron Slain?"

Ronan had to stop in his tracks to give Byron the appropriate look of disbelief. He was almost tempted to thump his crutches against the ground for extra emphasis.

"I meant Lord Byron," he said, "you know, the original goth. And your surname is Slain? As in 'murdered'? Were you deliberately aiming for the most edgy name possible?"

"I have no idea what you're talking about," Byron said, "I got it from one of those word games where the letters are all jumbled up."

"I don't believe you."

"I did!"

"I don't believe that, and I don't believe that you don't know who Lord Byron was! He was friends with Mary Shelley! You know, the woman who wrote *Frankenstein!*" Ronan awkwardly held up a hand when Byron opened his mouth to reply. "If you start to say any variation on 'that's a movie' I will never kiss you again."

Byron laughed, and leaned forward to kiss Ronan's forehead in an intolerably condescending fashion.

"I know it was a book."

Rolling his eyes, Ronan nudged Byron's foot with his crutch, but not hard enough to put Byron off kissing him again. "Come on. There has to be more to this story than 'you just saw some random letters and made them your name'."

"It's a long story."

"I have nothing but time."

6

It had been the week after his eighteenth birthday.

His parents had bought him a high-end laptop, a new phone, and an unnecessarily sophisticated suitcase.

He hadn't thought much about the last gift.

David and Gianna never really seemed to know what they were doing when it came to presents, or things for him in general. They were convinced that too much stimulation was the source of his 'behavioral problems,' so he rarely received anything exciting.

Still, a new laptop was good. It was rare for him to get technology that was all his own.

He should have been suspicious when Gianna kept talking about its video chat capabilities over dinner, but he'd been so happy just to be out of the house he hadn't noticed her odd focus on the subject.

They'd taken him to New York, for dinner and a show.

They said it was to 'make up' for the incident at his birthday party. Ben thought it was to make him forget the terrible, but true, things Marco had said to him after a drink too many; or when the ambulance came to take Star away for reasons that had already slipped his mind. The man had been bleeding, at the bottom of the stairs, but Ben couldn't remember why. Perhaps he'd never known.

Whatever the reason, the meal had been good. The show, less so. He'd wanted to see a comedy but Gianna had insisted that it wasn't appropriate, so they'd seen Phantom of the Opera instead. Ben hadn't really enjoyed that – he knew what happened in the end. When he was small, he'd dreamed of being a hero, but the older he got the more he empathized with the bad guy.

He had still been looking forward to the next day, at least. There had been the promise of brunch and sightseeing, but Gianna got a call, as always, so they'd headed back to D.C. at midnight.

Ben would rather be there than back at their house in the Hamptons – with its awful memories, and the horrible summer house – but he was getting far too tall to sleep comfortably in the back of the car.

Which was why he was awake enough at 3am to hear David say, "Are you sure this is the best thing for him? There's nothing there!"

"Precisely."

"No, scratch that, there's nothing there but planes and aviation fuel."

Gianna sighed. "He hasn't started a fire in years."

"If he messes with aviation fuel there won't be a fire, there'll just be a smoking crater where your brother's compound used to be."

There was an uncomfortable pause before David continued, "And what about college?"

"Do you really think Ben is going to go college? Ever? He's not stable enough, David, we can't risk…"

"He's a smart kid!"

"Maybe one day," Gianna said in that tone mothers have, the one that means 'never.' "Taking a break won't harm him, and working for Marco is just the sort of character-building colleges look for, especially given his educational history. No Ivy League school is going to take someone who went to so many 'specialist' schools unless they can prove they're exceptional."

'Specialist schools.' Ben hated that phrase. Just call them what they were – institutions for the mentally unstable. Military school, boarding school, anger management camp. The intention had always been the same. To fix the broken kid.

"Yeah, you're right," David said. "Maybe in ten years he can go to a local community college or something."

Gianna hummed but said nothing.

Ben stared out of the car window, wondering what to do.

Ben climbed out of the window and crept carefully down the fire escape.

He didn't need to – Gianna had been at work all night, and David had vanished like he usually did. The staff wouldn't notice or care if Ben left, they always did their best to pretend he didn't exist.

But climbing out the window was the traditional start to running away from home.

He'd often thought about doing this, when he'd been stuck scrubbing floors with a toothbrush for answering back or standing in the rain for hours as punishment for getting into a fight that he hadn't even been involved in.

But he'd never been in a position to follow through.

Running away as a child hadn't made sense to him.

The idea had always come to him when he was already in a shitty situation – ending up living on the street didn't seem all that much better. He was a tall, lanky kid with really distinctive features and very powerful parents. He'd have been hauled home in days unless he hid really well, and living in the woods really wasn't his style. So, he'd put up with things. But he'd done some quiet research when he could.

Now he wasn't a child anymore.

He was an adult, and he was going to make his own way in the world.

Gianna had always kept a bank account for him. It wasn't a joint account – it was entirely his, she'd just never given him the documents. It contained eighteen years of birthday and holiday gifts from generous friends and relatives who'd been quietly told not to buy him physical things in case they induced an 'episode.'

He'd seen the documents once, in her safe.

Conveniently they were kept with his passport; driver's license (which he'd been allowed to obtain at the earliest possible age but never permitted to use); birth certificate; and Social Security documents. Everything he needed, as an adult, to live an independent life.

Unsurprisingly, the safe had been locked, and Gianna would never, ever have told him the combination. But it was the old style, with the turning lock; it was easy for him to put a hand on the door and feel when the lock wanted to open. He'd always wondered why other people didn't just do the same.

Taking the bundle of documents that were legally his own property still felt oddly like stealing. He didn't feel guilty about it, not really, just a strange kind of uncomfortable that made his skin prickle.

If anything, leaving the note was even harder. It felt like beginning a trail of breadcrumbs when he didn't really want to be found, or a cry for attention when he wanted none.

But he couldn't just leave.

Not with his mother's position in the government, or shadowy hints about his father's business. Leaving without a word would lead to a manhunt.

His face would be all over the news with a scrolling ticker tape of hysteria underneath. *CEO makes tearful plea for return of kidnapped son.* He hated what Gianna had done in the name of helping him, but not enough to do that to her in return.

He started the note a dozen times. 'Dear Mom': no. 'To Mom & Dad': no. 'Greetings parental units': good god, no, what the fuck was he thinking? 'Gianna': no.

In the end no salutation worked so he just dove straight in–

"I won't go to Ohio. I want to live my own life. I'll do my best not to embarrass you anymore. Please don't look for me. Ben."

He left it tucked inside Gianna's day planner where the staff wouldn't see it, but she would hopefully find it before she even realized he'd gone. It was the best he could do.

He'd thought about running away often, but he'd never had a plan.

All kinds of grandiose ideas had come to him while he made his way to Union Station – he could go to Los Angeles and become a star; he could go to Florida and get a job at a theme park; he could go to Hawaii and sleep on a beach as far away from the Hamptons as he could possibly get – he could have gone anywhere, and been anything.

He was a grocery bagger in an independent supermarket on the outskirts of Chicago.

It wasn't glamorous, but no one would think to look for him here.

Getting a job had been harder than he thought. He was living in a motel, with no previous history and no references.

After eight interviews, he'd become frustrated by the number of questions people asked for the most basic of roles.

Finally, at his ninth interview, he'd snapped, "Why don't you just give me the fucking job?"

His boss – a nice lady called Sofia who was just trying to run the market singlehanded since the death of her husband – had blinked and said in a monotone, "Why don't I just give you the flipping job?"

"You want to give me the job?" Ben had asked, suddenly confused at her tone.

"Yes, I want to give you the job."

A trickle of blood had run from her nose as she spoke, and Ben felt a little sick.

As quickly as the change came, she seemed to recover, though she was still a little disoriented as she shook hands with him and showed him around.

He hadn't known exactly what he'd done, but he'd resolved to be the best damn bagger he could be. The hours were shit, the pay was shit, the work was shit, but it was better than nothing.

He spent his time off at the motel, bored out of his mind with only the internet for company. Though he soon found things online that would help change his outlook on life.

He'd always been good at the physical elements of military training, even if everything else had been beyond him – a search for ways to improve the heavy-lifting at his job had led him to a forum dedicated to bodyweight exercises. He couldn't afford fancy equipment, but he had a doorframe, and gallon jugs of milk. That was all he needed.

Six months after leaving home Ben was sure no one would recognize him anymore.

He'd added twenty pounds of muscle, thanks to the tips and encouragement he'd gotten online, and now his hair covered some of his face, so he felt much more comfortable in his own skin. Still out of place, but better.

His change in size had hidden benefits, too.

"Hey, man," he said casually to a regular customer, "I think you wanna take that stuff out of your back pockets. You must have forgotten to pay for it."

He was getting better at giving a little push to his words, just enough to make people want to take his lead, but even the ones who resisted saw the muscles stretching the sleeves of his uniform and gave in.

"Dude, you should be working in loss prevention," the cashier whispered gratefully.

Ben laughed, but filed it away to research later.

It was six months after his nineteenth birthday that Ben heard the music for the first time.

He was in a mall, shopping for something that might pass for professional enough to get him through the interview with a security company, when he passed a store that he'd never really paid attention to before.

Music hadn't really been a part of his life. David had listened to his terrible dad rock in the car, and Gianna had favored classical music when she needed to concentrate, but anything else had been deemed too exciting for Ben. Not just music – movies, television, books – he had so much catching up to do now that he was a free man.

He'd stood in front of the store listening to the music for so long that security had asked him if he was high. Too embarrassed to come up with an excuse, he'd made them go away and hurried inside.

He enjoyed the next song just as much as the first – it spoke to his pain more than anything else had in his entire life. He felt like the songwriter knew him, personally, and had written every word just for him. Listening to that music felt like not being alone for the first time in a decade.

The young man behind the counter smiled sweetly despite all his piercings when Ben asked what the song was called. The smile made Ben blush.

Four hours later Rhydian was making Ben blush in an entirely different way.

Ben was out of the motel, but he hadn't managed to furnish his studio yet, not with what he earned as a security guard at the grocery store. His savings were traceable – he wasn't ready to risk being found by using that money more than necessary. So, his room was just a mattress on the floor and a sheet thrown over the curtain rail for privacy.

Rhydian didn't care. He'd just wanted to get his hands on Ben, and Ben had just wanted to let him.

That was an afternoon of firsts. Ben would have been lying if he said he hadn't had some hurried experiences with other boys at the various schools he'd attended, but he'd never gone so far before.

Ben had never been kissed like this, or felt lust like this. He'd never done any of the things Rhydian so carefully showed him. But it was the fact that Rhydian stayed that surprised him most.

He'd never laid in someone's arms and shared a clove cigarette while the other person talked about music, life, and fashion. He'd never received an enthusiastic blowjob then been allowed to linger in bed just for the sake of lingering. He'd never thought you could take the time to get to know someone like this.

The next morning when Rhydian mentioned being thirsty, Ben had fetched him a bottle of water from the mini fridge without thinking about it. He didn't get up to do so. He didn't need to, and he'd lived alone for so long. Until now there was no one to panic at the fact that he could just reach out a hand and pull something to him without touching it.

Rhydian had stared, wide eyed.

Ben had braced for the screaming to start.

Instead his companion lit his next cigarette with a fingertip and blew a dragon-shaped cloud of smoke at the ceiling.

Rhydian broke Ben's heart in less than a year, but he'd taught Ben so much that he could never really find it in his heart to hate him. Even when he claimed to be a two-thousand-year-old warlock trapped in a perpetually young body. Ben had heard and seen a lot of strange things over the years, but he recognized a bullshit reason to break up when he heard one.

They both knew he'd made up the age gap instead of just admitting that he'd been cheating on Ben with the cute girl from the donut stand.

Still, it had been Rhydian who suggested leaving an offering of cream to the local spirits for good luck. That little trick had landed Ben a job paying four times his previous wage.

Ben owed a lot of his personal style to him, too – not just the skinny jeans and band t-shirts, or the hair and piercings – it had been Rhydian who had shown him that there was more to this world than mundane society might think.

And it was Rhydian who encouraged Ben to practice his skills and push the boundaries of what he thought he could do. Such as starting a fire in the underwear of a cheating boyfriend from forty feet away.

Just because Ben could never bring himself to hate Rhydian didn't mean he wasn't angry.

He was heading west on the old Route 66 just outside of Albuquerque when a bird hit the windshield of his shitty Oldsmobile. Between blood and broken glass, visibility was reduced to zero and the car ended up in a ditch.

He climbed shakily out to check the damage and found his eye drawn back along the road.

It was a big fucking bird.

It was a black man-sized bird, with a bald head and a white ruff of feathers that were stained with blood and gravel.

No. It was a man. He was covered in blood, a few feathers, and an epic case of road burn, but not much else. Just a naked middle-aged man, laying in the road.

Ben looked at the damage to his car. The first impact point was definitely at the top of the windscreen. Nothing but the wall of the ditch had hit the grille, and the hood looked like its usual rusty self.

Ben looked around.

There was nothing near him.

He counted four tumbleweeds in the distance and a couple of scraggly bushes, but there was nothing above knee height. Certainly, no trees that the man could have fallen out off. There was a telegraph line running alongside the service road, but there was no way a human could leap that kind of distance.

Ben looked up. Surely anyone falling from a plane would have been going fast enough to cause a hell of a lot more damage to his car. Either way, the dawn sky was clear.

"Mother*fucker*!"

Well, at least he didn't have a dead body to explain to the police. However much radio silence he'd had from Gianna and David, *that* certainly would have gained their attention.

He walked around to the back of the car and punched the lock in just the right way to make it open. There was a black velvet duster that would probably survive the bloodstains better than his other clothes.

Ben stared off to one side as he approached the man who was now laid on his back and swearing at the sky. He had no problem with the naked body, but most people didn't like to be looked at without consent, and Ben had no idea how this guy would react. Besides, the sight of that much gravel burn was making his eyes water.

"Hey man, can you stand?" Ben asked, "Do you want me to get you to a hospital, or should I call an ambulance?"

"Don't call a fucking ambulance, are you stupid or something?" The man looked up at Ben and sneered. "Oh god, you are. Do I look like I need a fucking ambulance?"

"Well your arm's broken and you're bleeding from approximately eighty percent of your skin, but you know what? – fuck you." Ben turned to walk away just as the man looked at his own arm and swore again.

"Hey get back here you little shit, you hit me with your fucking car!"

"Best I can tell – you dropped from the sky onto my fucking car! I offered you help, you gave me insults, you wanna try again?"

The man made a noise that sounded oddly like a pissed-off bird of prey. "I guess you can take me to the hospital," he said as he sat up.

"Lucky me," Ben said. "Here, put this on."

Another look of contempt, this time directed at the coat in Ben's hands. "Hell no!"

"No offense, but I don't want your blood-smeared naked ass on my seats."

"A lot of fucking offense but your car is a piece of shit, besides, I ain't queer enough to wear that get up and I've been living with my boyfriend for fifteen fucking years."

Ben went back to the car and dragged an item from the trunk. It wasn't actually his, he was transporting it cross-country for a friend who was really into amateur theatre, but it was hilarious to watch the man's face when the huge glittery pink skirt of Glinda The Good Witch's dress flowed into view.

"Pick one," he said with a nasty grin.

"So," Ben said conversationally, as they drove past a police car at five miles under the speed limit. Somehow neither officer inside noticed the missing windshield. "Do you have a name, or should I just call you Mr Homophobia Death-Wish?"

"Fuck you, I ain't phobic. I just think you look like an asshole."

"Sure thing, Mr Death-Wish."

The man stuck his nose in the air. "Shut up. My name's Woodburn."

"First or last?"

"Woodburn Cole."

"Oh my god, that's the most made-up name I've ever heard," Ben laughed. "Look, if you don't wanna tell me, fine. You wouldn't be the first half-naked guy I've had in this car that didn't tell me his real name."

"Jesus, kid, have some self-respect. How old are you? Twenty-six?"

Ben shrugged, the amused expression melting from his face. "I'm nineteen. Twenty next month."

"Oh god."

After that Woodburn said nothing except to quietly direct him to the nearest hospital.

Given that the man was still mostly naked, Ben went inside to find a nurse – the first one he encountered seemed to know Woodburn by name. She didn't react to his lack of clothes as she led him to a bed, though perhaps she couldn't tell under the coat he kept tight around himself. He was a lot thinner than Ben, so there was plenty of fabric to keep him covered.

He would get treated, Ben had done his duty, and given up on the coat as a lost cause, so he turned to leave. "See ya! I'd better go find a mechanic to fix my car."

"No, you stay with me," Woodburn called out. "I'll see you right."

It was more than a little uncomfortable sitting next to a stranger in a backless hospital gown who clearly knew most of the hospital staff. The longer he sat there, the more Ben worried about someone noticing the blood on his car and alerting the police. He could distract them when they were in front of him, but he'd yet to work out a way to make something invisible at a distance.

An elderly Asian doctor with an oddly foxish haircut spoke to Woodburn for a few minutes in hushed tones. Ben tried not to eavesdrop and found himself staring at a point just behind her. He almost jumped in his seat when a pure white bushy tail swished out of her long coat for a moment before vanishing.

Maybe Ben should get checked out for a concussion of his own. He'd heard of fox spirits in the past, but he'd never met anyone with 'extra' abilities who wasn't human. Not that he had met all that many people who could do the things he could do – after Rhydian he'd learned to be more discreet – but to meet one working in an emergency room in the middle of the desert? That seemed very unlikely.

"I'll order you some x-rays so we can get that arm set properly," she was saying when he looked up at her. She seemed completely normal so he must have been imagining things. "And you need a sight test. It's a highway, Woodburn, you keep flying that low with shitty eyesight, you're going to hit the power lines."

As she left, Ben heard Woodburn mutter a comment about 'wearing glasses on a beak,' but he didn't understand what he meant. Maybe it was a hang-gliding term or something.

"I heard that!" she called back from the doorway. "Get laser surgery like everyone else!"

Awkward silence returned.

"Look, don't worry about my car, I'll sort it out myself," Ben began.

"Shut up," Woodburn snapped, then sagged. "Jesus, you shouldn't have to do anything. I was pissed off, I thought you were older than you are, but she's right – I shouldn't have been so low over the highway even this early in the morning. You're just a kid, you shouldn't have to pay for my mistake."

The man sighed, looking away and rubbing awkwardly at his bald scalp. That was the most words he'd said to Ben in one go. The effort seemed to have exhausted him.

Just when Ben was trying to frame a question about hang-gliding, or paragliding, or however the man had ended up crashing into his car, Woodburn looked at him again.

"You never did tell me your name, boy."

"Ben. Ben Franklin."

Woodburn narrowed his eyes.

"Okay, fine, it's Ben Williams," Ben shrugged. He rarely gave his real name out, unless he wanted to get paid or rent a place to live. He tried to keep his identity as quiet as possible, even if – as far as he knew – his parents had never made an effort to find him.

"No, that's not right," Woodburn said. "That sits on you like a blanket, that's not your soul's name."

Ben didn't really know how to respond to that. He wasn't even sure he had a soul.

"I didn't name me," he said as neutrally as he could.

"Maybe you should," Woodburn replied. When Ben just stared at him, he changed the subject. "Look. I'm a mechanic, I own a shop out towards Petroglyph. Your car is fucked. Replacing the windshield is gonna cost you more than the car is worth. But I've got a few old trucks I took in trade, one of those might suit you."

"I can't afford–" Ben protested. Technically he *could* afford a new car with money in his savings, but he still didn't want to touch it. And besides, the Oldsmobile ran, it just...didn't have a windshield anymore. Provided he covered that up when he parked for the night, he'd make it to California.

"I don't expect you to pay me! I wrecked your car; I owe you a new one."

She was beautiful.

She was the single most gorgeous thing he'd seen in his entire life.

She was an epiphany.

He'd always considered himself to be gay but now he knew he was wrong.

This car was his sexuality.

"You're really fucking weird, kid," Woodburn said in a disgusted tone.

They were standing on the back of his lot, staring at a car. Well, to Ben she was a car. Woodburn had described her as a heap of rusting junk.

"That thing ain't gonna run," Woodburn went on, rolling his eyes when Ben failed to move on to the truck he'd intended to show him.

His mood hadn't improved now that his arm was in a cast, but at least he was finally dressed in the grease-stained overalls his partner had brought to the hospital. Atherton hadn't seemed all that surprised about the incident, though he had agreed that Woodburn did indeed owe Ben a new vehicle.

"But could she be repaired?" Ben asked quietly. For some reason he felt like he was insulting her with his question.

"Well...yeah? Anything can be rebuilt eventually," Atherton said as he ran his fingers over a grey beard that almost looked blue against his skin tone. "It needs most of a new engine, new suspension, reupholster and respray, but, technically, yeah, any car will run if you put enough work in. Isn't worth it though."

Ben looked at the two skinny men – both of them in later middle age, one with his arm in a sling – and then looked pointedly around the lot. "Do you guys need an apprentice? One who can do a lot of heavy lifting? You can pay me in lessons on how to fix that car..."

They looked skeptically at him, then at the car.

"You do know that's a first-generation Plymouth Fury, right?" Atherton asked. "Have you read that book? 'Cos you look like the sort of goth creep that probably has."

Ben narrowed his eyes. "I see you're just as charming as he is. Yeah, I've seen the movie. Don't worry, I won't paint her red, with either paint or blood."

"Really fucking creepy."

"Yeah, well," Ben snapped back, "a naked guy fell on my car this morning, I'm not having the greatest of days."

She was beautiful, but she was a total wreck. If anything, Atherton had wildly underestimated the amount of work she needed.

In a way that just made Ben love her even more.

He would have said that they were kindred spirits, but Woodburn would probably have called him a melodramatic asshole if he'd said that out loud.

Still, it was satisfying to work on her for an hour at the end of a day. He could zone out, real peaceful-like, and let his brain wander while his hands did all the work. It was almost like that mediation thing his therapists had tried to help him with for years. Though sadly, just like in therapy, no matter how peaceful he felt, the anger was always lurking below the surface.

Today he was fighting with the glove compartment, which was jammed shut by years of rust and what looked like pigeon droppings.

"Come on, darling," he muttered soothingly while he tried to fit the crowbar into the space above the lock. "The sooner we get you clean, the sooner we can get you fixed. The sooner you're fixed, the sooner you're back on the road where you belong. Come on, for Ben, please?!"

The crowbar slipped, cutting into his thigh.

"Ah, you bitch!" He kicked the dashboard.

The glove compartment dropped open. Out tumbled a bunch of mildewed papers, a travel board game, and approximately one hundred angry bees.

"Waaaaaaaah!"

He threw himself out of the car and scrambled towards open ground.

At the edge of the yard he could just see Atherton and Woodburn pause in talking to a customer.

"Bees!" he shouted, throwing up his hands in an effort to keep the insects away. He'd never tried to create a bubble around himself, he'd always just moved individual objects, but there were far more bees than he could possibly concentrate on.

He was soaked in sweat and had been stung in a few places by the time he'd managed to make a safe sphere of empty space with him in the center.

"Well, that's a neat trick," Atherton said flatly, from surprisingly close by.

Ben jumped. "Shit! You shouldn't have got so close; you could have been stung!"

The other man made a noncommittal noise, and gestured towards the house. "Go get a shower and count your stings – if it's more than ten we should get you to the emergency room. Woodburn and me will deal with the bees."

"You're gonna call an exterminator?"

"Yeah, something like that."

It was probably the condensation on the bathroom window, or the steam in the air, that made Ben think he could see man-sized birds moving around the yard while he showered.

He hadn't hit his head, or suffered an allergic reaction, so an optical illusion was the only sensible explanation for what looked like two giant birds hopping around the Fury.

One of the birds was grey-blue. The other had a white ruff of feathers around its neck.

Something shifted with a meaty noise, and he saw his bosses sitting naked by the now bee-free car instead.

Yeah, that was a sight that needed more of an explanation than steam. Maybe the shampoo in here was hallucinogenic, or he'd developed a brain tumor in the last ten minutes.

Or perhaps he was the most oblivious man alive, and his bosses were shapeshifting werebirds.

Which would have explained the whole falling from the sky and landing on his car thing.

Also, the comments about 'flying.'

And the fox who worked at the hospital.

Damn.

Ben had been working here for an entire month now. There was absolutely no way he could say anything to them at this point – they already thought he was stupid.

He'd just be proving them right.

Better to keep his mouth shut about that one.

"Hey," Ben said to the car when he was absolutely certain no one was looking, "I'm sorry I called you a bitch. And I'm sorry I kicked you. I totally deserved the bees."

He patted the dashboard gently, then recoiled in fright when another object dropped from the glove compartment. He couldn't face any more bees today.

It was just another piece of the board game that had fallen out the day before. It was one of those games where you had to make words out of random letters. Gianna had tried to interest him in educational games when he was younger, but he'd always found them boring. That, and the temptation to spell rude words was just too much for a teenage boy to resist. He'd never needed another reason for her to be mad at him.

He reached down to clean it up and then stopped.

There were a few dozen or so pieces scattered across the rotten carpet. Three of them spelled out his name.

Ben glanced around, half wondering if someone sinister had left him a message, like in movies when people cut words out of magazines. Of course, he was alone, because that was a crazy idea.

When he looked at the tiles again, he realized he could read more than one name amongst the letters – BENQRTBYRONKSLAIN. He laughed to himself. Imagine how freaked out he would have been if his surname had been Slain, or Byron.

Patterns appear everywhere in life. This was just a random collection of letters.

Nothing more.

"Hiiii..."

Why did all the best-looking guys work in weird alternative clothing stores? Ben wondered if it was something in the combined smell of patchouli and vinyl clothes that attracted them. To be honest, that and the music always drew him in, whether he had the funds to buy anything or not.

Rhydian had been an average-build guy who just looked tall thanks to his Mohawk. This one was tiny, with dreadlocks that faded to sunset colors at the ends and lips that looked like they could be kissed for days.

"What's your name?"

Ben opened his mouth to reply, and for reasons he couldn't possibly explain, he said, "Byron."

"Nice. Well met, Byron," the guy replied in a voice so divine that he didn't even think of correcting him.

It was strange, but somehow it felt right on his tongue.

A week later so did his new boyfriend.

He'd placed a dish of cream on the Fury's dashboard in thanks. The next day he discovered that the wiring in the car wasn't nearly as bad as expected, saving him a few hundred dollars.

Unfortunately for him the cream soon went bad under the desert sun, but he'd learned to adapt. The Fury – she didn't need any other name – would be a beautiful car once she was fixed, so he brought her beautiful things. Flowers that grew by the roadside, plastic jewelry from the dollar store, the occasional huge feather he found behind the car lot – she didn't seem to mind, as long as it was delivered with a little bit of ceremony.

Despite his realization about his shapeshifting bosses, Byron couldn't bring himself to see the gifts as more than a superstitious ritual – a car was just an inanimate object, it couldn't give you a name, or attack you with bees – but once he started, he found that he couldn't stop. He didn't want to stop.

The way Rhydian had put it, you were supposed to give gifts to the spirits of your home, and you had to love your home if you wanted the spirits to stay. That was what made it a home in the first place.

The car wasn't a house, it hadn't been built as a home, but for Byron that's what it was, even long before he got it back on the road.

7

"IT'S A GOOD THING YOU'RE NOT THE SORT OF PERSON WHO DOES anagrams for fun," Ronan said when Byron's story seemed to have wound its way to an ending.

"I don't think that person exists," Byron laughed, though he was frowning as if he didn't understand what Ronan meant.

"Those letters you found – you could have lots of other names than the ones you read in sequential order! You could have been Alien Boners. Or Bison Leaner. Nobby Tinkler. If you wanted a really weird name you could have called yourself Strain Brokenly or Antlike Snobbery... Actually, no, that one has too many Bs."

Judging by the look on Byron's face, he didn't find this nearly as amusing as Ronan did.

"Of course, you can't do much with a Q if you don't have a U," Ronan went on, determined to continue digging this hole now that he'd started. "Though if you added a D you could be Beyond Brains."

"Oh, I bring the D all right," Byron said flatly, "and I'm an expert at using it to take you beyond your brain."

"And your ego isn't massive at all."

They stared at each other, both trying to keep their expressions entirely humorless.

Ronan broke first.

He just couldn't get the thought of a man called Nobby Tinkler out of his mind.

As soon as he began laughing, Byron cracked too. Once they started it felt like they couldn't stop until Ronan was half hanging out of his chair and gasping for breath.

"Oh my god, I needed that."

Byron snorted. His expression was turning pensive now. He kept looking at the shadows cast by his fingers as he flexed them one-by-one.

Ronan wasn't sure how long they'd been talking – he'd barely even noticed them sitting down – but the shadows were starting to get longer. They must have been in the hospital garden for ages.

"Did you actually listen to any of what I said after I talked about the letters, or were you too distracted 'having fun' with anagrams?" Byron asked. He made the biggest air quotes possible around having fun, which Ronan found a little offensive. There was nothing wrong with word games to pass the time.

"No, I can multitask. You ran away from home, you met some guys, hit one of them with your car, had several personal awakenings and developed some kind of obsession with a different car," Ronan said. He resisted the urge to count the bullet points on his fingers as he normally would. He didn't want Byron to think he was mirroring him just to make fun of him.

"I'm not sure I understand why you didn't realize Woodburn was a bird when you hit him though? I mean, obviously shock can mess with your head, but…"

Byron shrugged as Ronan trailed off, unable to think of a way to ask the question without implying anything about Byron's thought process, or lack thereof.

When he failed to break the silence, Ronan added, "You were very insistent about the werewolf."

"I've learned a lot since then, like how to trust my own eyes." As Byron spoke his shoulders curled in like he was instinctively shielding himself from something. "I spent most of my childhood being told that what I thought I saw or felt was wrong. I guess it was too much of a leap to get straight to 'shapeshifters are real.' I didn't even know all the things *I* could do then."

In an effort to lighten the mood, Ronan said, "Like start fires with your mind."

On the other side of the lawn a window opened. Byron looked towards the sound, but Ronan couldn't tell if that was a reflexive movement or just an excuse not to look at him anymore.

"Are you bothered by that?"

"If you only set cheaters on fire, I can promise you I'd never do that."

Byron nodded but didn't turn to face him.

"I, uh, Ben might have embellished things a bit, to make himself seem cool," Byron said in a weirdly stilted tone. Either he was blushing or the sunset had arrived sooner than usual. "There weren't tons of guys in that car – the Oldsmobile, I mean – I didn't get the confidence to do things like that until after I got the Fury. That boy with the dreadlocks, Jordan, he was the one that bought me eyeliner, and shaved my undercut for the first time. He took me to concerts, and showed me off. In nightclubs thoughts are loud, lust is louder... I went a little wild after we broke up."

Since he still wasn't looking in his direction, Ronan placed a reassuring hand on Byron's knee. He knew a thing or two about going wild himself – it was a natural consequence of a restricted upbringing – but now wasn't the time to share all that.

"I'm clean!" Byron said suddenly. "Health-wise I mean, I've always been careful, I get tested. I've never really done drugs, and getting drunk is just...whatever, but I need you to know, I'm not...normal. In the head."

Ronan debated responding with one of about a dozen witty comebacks, but he wasn't a complete arsehole, so instead he stood awkwardly from his chair to kiss Byron's cheek.

"Normal is overrated."

Byron turned his face enough to kiss him back.

"I made up the extra letters between Ben, Byron, and Slain you know," he said, once Ronan came up for air. "I'm not a nerd like you, I'm not going to remember random game pieces from eight years ago."

"I beg your pardon? I am not a nerd," Ronan huffed, stepping away toward the door that would lead to their room.

He was stopped by a hand on his wrist almost instantly. Before he could say anything else, Byron had tugged him gently down to sit across his knee.

"You do anagrams – you're a nerd."

It was such a childish argument. Ronan had been an officer. He was thirty-five, seven years Byron's senior if he had his maths right. He should behave like an adult.

He stuck his tongue out.

Just as he'd expected, Byron tried to bite it, and then turned the gesture into a needlessly vigorous kiss.

Ronan had had enough of being sensible for a while. Right now, he'd rather have fun.

"You ran away from home," Ronan began quietly that night, when the lights were out and Byron was half dozing against his chest. "You ran away, but you said it was your father who admitted you under the wrong name, and it was your cousin who stabbed y–"

"I wouldn't call it a stabbing," Byron mumbled.

"What else would you call a sword going through your shoulder? A skewering? Accidental perforation?"

"Unplanned hardcore piercing?"

Ronan snorted. "Whatever. It was your cousin who unintentionally penetrat–"

"No! Nope! Stop talking! Don't finish that word, I don't want to think about Darcey in connection to that word!"

Since Byron had already covered Ronan's mouth with his hand finishing the sentence wasn't really an option. Though Ronan was mildly tempted to think the words at him loudly, just to get a rise out of him, but that wouldn't have been playing fair.

He raised his hands to show he'd relented.

Byron peered up at him through the perpetual curtain of hair with suspicion, so Ronan kissed his palm to add a little more reassurance.

"She'll always be my baby cousin..." He didn't finish the statement but the meaning was clear.

Ronan asked his next question as tactfully as he could, he didn't want to insult someone Byron clearly cared about. "Do you know why she hasn't visited you?"

"She got hurt too, but not as bad. I needed surgery, she didn't. So, different hospitals. She was released after a day. But walking around with burns sucks, and she's forever texting me." It was hard to tell with his face half covered but Ronan was sure he saw Byron wink. "She hasn't visited because she doesn't want to cramp my style."

As if the hint wasn't enough Byron slid a hand down Ronan's side to squeeze as much of his ass as he could reach.

"Classy."

"Yeah, she's great."

"What about your parents?"

Byron's hand immediately returned to its resting position on the bed.

"David and Gianna are busy," he said flatly. "They're always busy. We, uh, we have an uneasy truce these days."

Ronan nodded, even though with his head back on Ronan's chest Byron probably couldn't see the gesture. Still, he knew better than to say anything on the subject – families were hard at the best of times – and pushing too much wouldn't help either of them. Byron had already opened up a lot today, it was better to let him take his time.

Thinking of time, Ronan suddenly realized that he didn't know how much of this they had left. He'd avoided the question of what came next to focus on healing, and getting to know the man beside him.

"I'm going to be discharged soon," Byron said quietly. Ronan shivered a little at the answering of a question he hadn't asked yet, though he didn't complain about the eavesdropping. It made sense that Byron had heard that thought, after all, it had made his own chest turn cold with worry. "I should have been out already but–"

"You decided to do some light furniture rearranging?"

"And I was pushing you all around the basement."

"Hey, I mostly wheeled myself! You only helped with the running parts."

"Which everyone knows is the easiest element of any monster hunt," Byron scoffed, then sighed. "What about you?"

"If they can find somewhere for me to stay, I should be released soon, too. I shouldn't be on my own for a while – so a hotel is right out – but I do need to be in an environment where I can get moving as much as possible. Problem is, they've got nowhere for me to stay and they won't approve me flying anywhere."

If Ronan was being honest with himself this situation was just as odd as him ending up in this hospital in the first place.

"You could stay with me."

The words were said so quietly, and muffled by his own collarbone, that Ronan wasn't entirely sure he'd heard them. When he looked down Byron still had his face pressed resolutely against his chest, so all he could see was the lighter caramel roots of his hair. Obviously, he'd realized the pink was dye but he hadn't expected the same of the black.

He shook his head, irritated at his own distraction.

"Did you just offer–"

"Yeah, you don't have to if you–"

"No, tell me more."

"You didn't mention stairs," Ronan said two days later, his tone distinctly unimpressed.

"It's not far," Byron murmured. As he spoke, he ran his left hand down over Ronan's ass. "We can do it together! See?"

Ronan's reply turned into a very undignified shriek of surprise when Byron hoisted him bodily up against his hip and practically ran up all five flights of stairs.

"What the fuck?" he gasped when he was finally deposited on the fifth-floor landing, Byron resting his face against his neck and panting heavily between giggles.

That should not have been possible. Ronan was a grown man, not a piece of weight-lifting equipment. He hadn't been carried like that since he was a toddler.

"Don't say you're not impressed," Byron all but purred, clearly very pleased with himself. Catlike, he licked Ronan's neck as if hauling him around like a sack of potatoes was a form of foreplay. "This is usually the point when people cling to me and swoon while their underwear sprouts wings and flies away."

Ronan narrowed his eyes. He might have been impressed if he'd been warned, or if Byron hadn't just told him he showed off like this for all his conquests. It was true that Ronan wouldn't have been able to climb the stairs himself, but his pride would have preferred to discuss the options first.

"You left our bags and my crutches downstairs," he said, pushing him back with fingertips against firm pecs that would have been tempting if they hadn't just embarrassed him. "They've probably been stolen by now."

Smirking, Byron sketched a bow. "Stay there, I shall return momentarily."

As he watched the huge man parkour his way back down the stairs, Ronan wondered why he could never seem to meet normal people. If he was this bad before they'd even reached his apartment, what would living with him be like?

After two minutes, when the sound of footsteps failed to return to the stairwell, he began to worry that the bags really had been stolen.

A ding sounded behind him.

"This way," Byron beckoned, the elevator door sliding closed as he dragged the last bag out into the corridor.

Why did he always end up with guys with a penchant for the dramatic?

"So, when I asked you if it was a two-bedroom apartment you didn't feel it necessary to point out that the second bedroom didn't actually contain a bed?" Ronan asked, mildly perturbed by the sheer volume of junk in the room in front of him.

It looked like a musical instrument store had crash-landed into the secret meeting place for a society of eldritch abominations. There were actual collections of paper scraps stuck to the walls and linked with colored string. Ronan had never seen the like of it outside a Hollywood movie.

"Well, I have a king-size, and we've been sharing a single-person hospital bed for the last week." Byron said, picking sadly at the door frame. "It didn't occur to me that you'd want to go back to sleeping on your own."

Guilt washed over Ronan at the desolation in his voice. They'd both had a hard day, and he'd let himself get wound up at having almost no clothes or supplies, and no support from the Ministry of Defence contacts who were supposed to be making this transition easier on him.

Now here he was making Byron feel just as abandoned but with the added insult of being in his own home.

"I haven't slept that well in years," Byron continued at almost a whisper.

"Oh hell, Byron, no," he said, catching Byron's face between his hands and turning him to look him in the eye. His scars had mostly closed now, still red and shiny but no longer at risk of reopening. Ronan ran a thumb soothingly over the skin beside them as he continued. "I just...I like you, I like you a lot. I was just expecting to have a space for myself, and my stuff – as little as I have right now. You know, I would still have said yes if you'd told me there was only one bed."

"Sorry." Byron had cheered up a little, but it wasn't the bright confidence he'd had on the stairs.

Ronan really needed to work on his patience while they settled into whatever their new routine was going to be. He knew he was more worried about being able to stay in the country than he was about Byron stretching the truth about his home. He shouldn't take that out on him.

Determined to put the smile back on Byron's face, Ronan went on coyly, "Besides, you really should at least buy me dinner before you try to get me into your bed. I'm not that easy, you know!"

"If you say so, General Deepthroat," Byron said with a mock salute.

"Thank you, Mr Slain," the delivery boy said, accepting a roll of bills that he didn't bother to check. "Ma was getting worried about you, she'll be happy to hear you're home again. You'll have to come into the restaurant though, and tell her what happened to your face."

Byron nodded vaguely in a way that seemed designed to make his hair fall forward. Was that a long-term habit to avoid eye contact when he was uncomfortable or something new to cover up his scars? Ronan should find the time to ask him, but right now he had a more immediate question.

"What's with the wodge of cash?" he asked, once Byron was carrying their dinner towards what might have been a table hidden under a pile of laundry. "You're not buying drugs, are you?"

"I told you I don't do that," Byron said without looking at him. "Why?"

"Dinner doesn't usually cost a few hundred dollars, and I'm not sure if you noticed but that guy had fox ears, I don't want–"

"Don't be racist. Speciesist. Whatever. Just because he's a kitsune, doesn't mean Donnie isn't a good kid. He probably didn't see you there so he didn't hide it. He kinda knows I can do stuff," Byron said, finally meeting Ronan's eye with a look of disappointment. "I was just paying for a month's worth of meals in advance – drunk me tends to be unable to find his wallet. Donnie's Ma took pity on me. So now I pay a set amount every month and she doesn't bother running a tab."

Ronan nodded slightly; his face flushed with embarrassment. "Sorry. I didn't mean it that way at all. Just, force of habit to be wary, I guess. I'm not used to, well, interacting with other folks that casually. There tends to be an element of seeking them out, they don't usually show up on the doorstep with food. I still don't get why you were freaking out about a werewolf when you lived with bird people and are friendly with fox spirits?"

"Because not everything that isn't human is good," Byron muttered darkly. "I've never seen a werewolf, or whatever you said Mac was – a Theremin? Does central D.C. look like prime wildlife habitat to you?"

"Therianthrope. A Theremin is a weird musical instrument. I get your point though. I've never really talked to a kitsune and just made a complete arse of myself so–"

Byron cut him off before he could finish. "It's not really comparable. Donnie was here doing his job; Mac was scrabbling at the door with razor sharp claws and murder in his eyes."

"True, but I just said something rude to you, outside of his hearing, and I won't do it again." Ronan poked him in the chest. "You barricaded our door shut and ripped your stitches in the process."

"'Oh, thank you for stopping your uncle from eating me, Byron, you're my hero'," Byron said in a singsong voice half to himself.

He was removing the covers from the food now and Ronan's stomach growled loudly as soon as the smell reached him.

"Are we actually angry with each other, or are we just hungry?"

Byron looked thoughtful for a moment.

"We could try eating and see if that helps," he said, gesturing for Ronan to follow him through onto the balcony.

The views across the city were far better than Ronan would have imagined. Their hospital window had shown them only the courtyard and other windows. He'd almost forgotten where they were until now.

There was a small table they could have eaten at, but it felt like a waste of the view not to lean against the chest-high railings while they ate. If that also meant they could lean against each other's shoulders rather than sitting across from one another, neither of them mentioned it.

They ate at a leisurely pace, Byron pausing now and then to point out the various sights and historical buildings, the tourist traps and best bars. Every location had a story. Usually wildly exaggerated and utterly hilarious, each tale was accompanied by dramatic hand gestures that morphed into gentle touches.

It felt a little like Byron was trying to convince himself that Ronan was really there. Trying to be subtle, Ronan moved closer to reassure him. Despite the muggy pre-storm weather, Byron's body heat was much more welcome than the humidity.

As his hunger faded Ronan realized he was relaxed in a way he rarely experienced on the ground.

It was the sort of feeling he got just after he stepped out of a plane, the total freedom of the void, nothing but the wind rushing through his hair and what felt like infinity compressed into a few brief minutes of flight. Except he never took risks with his parachute, no matter how tempting it might be in the moment to see just how long he could wait.

Despite everything – his wounds, the end of his military career, the uncertainty over his future – being with Byron felt like being in permanent free-fall. All the thrill of a skydive without the disappointment of reaching the ground.

Ronan was beginning to realize he'd never been in love before, and maybe this was what everyone else felt like. He wasn't sure if he should be concerned.

The setting sun was painting the city in shades of gold by the time Ronan finally came back to himself enough to realize that Byron was staring at him with a soft smile on his face. Both their take out boxes were empty. Ronan didn't even remember finishing his own. He had to assume the food had been good.

In his hands the box, and his fork, shifted slightly as if someone was tugging on them with a minimal amount of effort.

Seeing him notice the movement, Byron winked.

It was hard, several stories above the street, to release his grip and trust that the items wouldn't fall, but after a second tug Ronan let them go.

Watching something as mundane as take out containers drift lazily back into the apartment felt somehow stranger than most other supernatural manifestations he'd seen. Usually when he'd seen telekinesis in the past it had been to make a point, not to avoid doing chores.

When he looked back at Byron the soft smile had widened into something a little more lascivious.

"I knew you'd look amazing out here at sunset; this light is perfect for your hair," Byron said fondly, as he brought one hand up to brush a thumb along the line of Ronan's jaw. His beard was growing in thick now, the strands rasping slightly with every touch. "The gold and copper looks so much better now without the florescent lights of the hospital. You looked barely half alive. Now you look like a god of wildfires, glowing like–"

Ronan couldn't help it.

He laughed.

He knew that he shouldn't, that this was clearly an attempt to be romantic and impressive, but he just couldn't resist the urge to laugh.

To lessen any insult to Byron's ego – and to show he did actually appreciate the sentiment of the words – Ronan leaned in and kissed him, which also had the benefit of making him stop.

A lifetime of conditioning made it hard to take compliments about his strawberry-blond hair seriously. Any other features would have been fine, but still not deserving of flowery poetry.

Although there had been a time when his looks had fallen into the skinny twink stereotype, that wasn't who he was now. He knew what he looked like – he worked out but not enough to get muscular, he was wiry rather than proportionately-built for his height, where his skin wasn't brown from the desert sun he was so pale he was practically translucent, his hair was everything from blond at the temples to orange at the crotch, his–

"You know, you can shut *me* up with a kiss, and yet your inner monologue continues," Byron said, pushing him away with one hand against his chest. "It's not healthy to think about yourself like that."

Even as he was moving him back, his other arm had slipped around Ronan's back to rest against the base of his spine like Byron's body didn't entirely know what it wanted from him.

To keep himself from being bent backwards like some kind of ballroom dancer Ronan grabbed the hand on his chest and brought it to his lips.

"Sorry. And thank you," he said as he kissed Byron's knuckles. "I'm not used to receiving compliments on my looks anymore."

"Well, we'll have to fix that won't we?"

Ronan let his free hand drift over Byron's uninjured shoulder, tracing the hollow between bicep and deltoid muscles. Perhaps his mind was exaggerating but each of those muscles seemed thicker than Ronan's entire arm. He was never going to get a compliment when he was standing next to Byron.

There was another tattoo there, some long swirling banner covered in text he couldn't quite read in the failing light. He tried to concentrate on that rather than his unexpectedly depressing thoughts. Where was any of this coming from?

As if on cue his knees twinged, reminding him that he'd been standing here for over an hour, and he hadn't taken any medication since the morning. He knew that as soon as he moved the pain would come rushing back. Perhaps that was coloring his mood.

"Hey," Byron murmured, leaning forward to rest his forehead against Ronan's own. "Hey, listen. As long as you're standing beside me you can have a compliment any second you want. I thought you were hot when you showed up unconscious in the next bed with a tube still down your throat. I spent the first day you were there trying to work out how to ask you out."

"And you chose 'werewolf crisis'?" Ronan laughed. He hadn't managed to see his reflection those first few days in the hospital, but he must have looked terrible, so for Byron to still like him despite that...

"Do you want some compliments?" Byron said this in the same tone someone might use to offer candy.

Ronan just laughed harder.

"Hey, don't laugh at me, I've a dozen sincere heartfelt compliments right here." Byron winked again. "I measure my compliments in inches."

Byron slid his hand down just far enough under the waistband of Ronan's trousers to run a suggestive fingertip over the crack of his ass. When Ronan shivered at the sensation, Byron stepped forward to bring them crotch to crotch.

"Subtle, aren't you?"

"Absolutely not." Byron laughed as he shoved his hand further down to grab an entire handful of buttock.

"Bloody hell!" It was supposed to be an admonishment but it came out as an embarrassingly horny groan as Byron ground his hips against Ronan's own. Giving into temptation Ronan wrapped his arms around Byron's shoulders and pulled him in for an enthusiastic kiss.

He was certain his medication was wearing off now – it had been dampening his own responses ever since he woke up, and while they'd spent some satisfying nights together in hospital, he'd never actually gotten off himself. Now the weight of weeks without release seemed to be weighing him down just as much as it was driving him on. Whatever they did, he wasn't going to last.

In an effort to slow things even for a second, he broke the kiss to turn his attention to Byron's neck, tracing a line down to his shoulder with his tongue.

Byron rolled his hips in response, clearly as eager as he was.

"From sweet compliments to humping me in less than a minute?" Ronan muttered. "Classy."

"Verbal compliments weren't working, so I thought I'd go for a practical demonstration."

To highlight his point Byron kneaded at Ronan's arse with both hands as he went on.

"Take this for example, you fit perfectly in my hands so I can do *this*."

He should have been expecting another show of strength from Byron but Ronan still squeaked in surprise when he was hauled into the air and pinned against the wall that divided their balcony from the next one. Any protests he might have made were cut off by the return of Byron's lips.

'Can I fuck you?'

The words appeared in Ronan's head without the aid of his ears. No, they weren't words, not really, or maybe they were words augmented by something more.

Ronan didn't just hear Byron's voice asking the question – he felt the press of flesh against his own, and the long slow rhythm of what Byron intended to do with him.

He tried to bite his lip against the overwhelming sensation, but nipped Byron's tongue instead.

Byron just growled and redoubled his efforts.

Ronan tried to think at Byron, to get across the idea that he wouldn't last long enough for them to do that, but even the thought that he might come in his pants was enough to get him toe-curlingly close to release.

It was impossible to get his point across this way.

Intellectually he didn't want to risk coming so soon, not on their first night together, no matter how understanding he knew Byron would be. It was a matter of pride.

But Byron felt wonderful everywhere their bodies met, and he was so close. His body didn't care about his pride.

Out of other options Ronan reached up to grab a handful of Byron's hair, gently tugging him back.

Judging by the way he moaned and thrust up Byron had something of a hair pulling kink.

Ronan imagined a stop sign. A single simple image, one that wasn't colored by complex desires.

Byron pulled back enough to meet his eye and froze in place.

For a second Ronan worried that he might have offended him, but Byron just smiled and kissed him gently.

"I won't last that long," Ronan said, now that he could finally get the words out.

"I won't judge you – if you want to come, then come."

"As tempting as that is, I don't want that," Ronan sighed, trying to get his breathing from panting down to a more reasonable regularity. "For one – these are my only good clothes, and I don't want to be doing laundry in the afterglow. But second – you did promise you'd take me to bed."

"Did I?"

"Well, I said you had to buy me dinner, and you did, so…"

Byron chuckled, half under his breath and leaned in until his face was against Ronan's neck.

"We could do this, then go to bed and do it again," he suggested in a voice that clearly knew his argument wouldn't get him anywhere, but was determined to ask anyway.

"Oh, I have no objection to doing it twice. I still don't want to do laundry. Come on, Byron, I want to be naked with you, and take our time. No worrying about nurses walking in without knocking. Just us."

Ronan turned his head to kiss Byron's hair.

"Please."

There was an odd grumble of protest but Byron lowered him to the floor all the same.

Despite the care that was clearly put into the maneuver, the act of putting weight back onto his legs sent a shock up Ronan's spine. He'd only been an inch or two off the floor but he felt like he'd fallen from a height.

Fortunately, his arms were still around Byron's shoulder, or else he probably would have fallen, and that would have been even less dignified than coming in his pants like a teenager.

Instead of commenting Byron simply moved an arm around Ronan's waist.

It was a little awkward to get two grown men back through the balcony door, but Ronan realized there was an advantage to making frequent stops to navigate tight spaces.

"You can't complain we're going too fast and then immediately start kissing me like that," Byron muttered the fourth time they stopped. He didn't actually make a move to reduce their contact though, so Ronan figured they'd be all right.

8

QUIETLY SINGING A CLASSIC ROCK SONG TO HIMSELF RONAN STAGGERED
to the coffeemaker. He was in a great mood but he knew he'd crash soon if
he didn't get some caffeine and medication into his system before he began
the day.

Well, the afternoon.

His first night in Byron's apartment had been fantastic – and exhausting
– but now he needed coffee, and food, and to go shopping so he had more
than one change of clothes. Both his father and his regiment had shipped
him some of his effects, but so far neither package had made it to him.

Borrowing his boyfrie – borrowing Byron's clothes could be considered
cute and romantic, but only in the privacy of the apartment. Even Byron's
leggings were too big on Ronan's much thinner legs, and he hadn't found a
single shirt that didn't drape on him like he was a toddler in his dad's clothes.

Right now, he was making do with a pair of Byron's boxers with a knot
tied in the waistband to keep them from falling down.

Cute was fine in private, but Ronan would definitely prefer to keep a
little dignity in public.

Someone coughed behind him. It wasn't Byron because Ronan had
left him in bed, and this sound came from the direction of the living room.

Moving carefully enough that he wouldn't provoke anyone, Ronan
scanned the kitchen counters for a weapon as he turned on his heel towards
the source of the noise.

Sadly, there were only protein powder tubs and supplement bottles on
hand. If Byron owned any cooking knives, he didn't keep them in easy reach.

A tiny, older woman stood in the center of the living room, dressed
in an expensive suit that artfully complimented her olive skin and white

hair. She was flanked by two men whose entire appearance screamed 'bodyguard.' Especially the holstered handguns that were barely concealed by their jackets.

Ronan placed his hands wide on the counter behind him for both support and visibility.

"Who are you?" the woman asked. She had a smoke-roughened voice and an air of authority – cold but not outright hostile. Not yet.

"Well, since you're the one intruding into my home I could ask the same, but I think I can guess," Ronan said as dispassionately as he could. "You must be Gianna Williams. Well, my name is Major Ronan Cox, formerly of British Army Parachute Regiment. Either the British Embassy or my boyfriend can confirm my identity if you don't believe me."

"And why are you here?"

Ronan narrowed his eyes.

Because I'm fucking your son, he thought. Because I might be in love with him. Because I was in the bed next to him for weeks, as you would know if you'd visited him even once during his recovery.

Ronan knew better than to say any of that. He was never at his best before his coffee, and he resented being ambushed in his own home while wearing someone else's oversized underpants. He couldn't be trusted not to say everything he just thought out loud, so he delegated.

"Byron!" he called over his shoulder. "You have some visitors! At least two of them are armed, so please don't take your time!"

"Ben!" the woman yelled in the same direction.

That set Ronan's teeth on edge.

"There's no one called Ben here," he snapped, stressing the name before he turned back to her. "This is Byron's apartment. His and mine."

"I don't know who you are but this is not your apartment, and I will not have some stranger living in this apartment – that I pay for – giving my son access to prescription medications."

"Prescription medication? What are you–"

He hadn't noticed it before due to the distraction of the armed goons, but the room behind her was wrecked. The shelves were in chaos, couch cushions had been pulled open, and both their hospital bags had been emptied onto the floor. Beside the remains of yesterday's take-out were nearly a dozen orange pill bottles neatly arranged into rows.

Ronan saw red. "What the hell gives you the right to search through my belongings?"

Other than that brief moment of suspicion the day before, he had never seen or heard any indication that Byron abused narcotics. If anything, his surgeon had scolded him for taking less than he was prescribed.

"You can see I've had surgery," he went on, with a sharp gesture towards his legs and their still livid scars, "and even if you never bothered to visit, you must know that Byron–"

A massive hand gripped his shoulder gently, silencing him before he went any further.

Turning to look at Byron with relief, Ronan barely registered the gasp from Gianna. He assumed that she was offended by his tone.

Thankfully, Byron had managed to find some yoga pants. Since Ronan had left him sleeping – and had borrowed his underwear – he'd been a little concerned that a half-asleep Byron might wander into the argument naked.

Ronan needn't have worried – Byron looked wide awake and absolutely murderous.

"Why are you here?" he snapped at his mother, casually handing Ronan his trousers as he spoke.

The gesture was appreciated, but there was no dignified way for him to put them on, so Ronan let them hang at his side. In other circumstances he might have tried to cover himself with them, but she was the one intruding on their home. He didn't feel like being polite.

Gianna didn't respond to the question. She was just standing there with her mouth hanging open.

"You know you're not supposed to be here without calling ahead," Byron tried again, though his tone wavered slightly this time.

"Oh, Ben, your face!" she cried, with all the melodrama of a cheap rate soap opera star. "Your father said you'd be getting plastic surgery! He said you were fine!"

"I don't know why David said that, I haven't seen him."

Ronan thought it was probably safe to assume that Byron's father was getting all his information from Mac – and since he'd barely been able to look at either of them the last time they met he wouldn't have had accurate information to give. He didn't bother to say any of that though. They had promised Mac they wouldn't tell.

Beside him Byron was shaking his head, clearly trying to get his hair to cover his face, forgetting that he'd tied it back the night before.

Uncertain what else to do, Ronan took his hand. He was shaking.

"The hospital should never have let you home without finishing the job!" Gianna sounded horrified. "What did your surgeons say?"

Byron shrugged and looked at his arm. There had once been a tribal-style shoulder cap tattoo running from collarbone to bicep, but now the design was half obscured by scars.

"I think they were too busy focusing on the use of my arm to worry about my face," he said. "Besides, burns don't work like that."

"Okay, but–"

"Why are you here, other than to tell me that I'm even more ugly now? You already said I ruined my looks with tattoos and stretching my ears, what does it matter if my face looks like a road map now?"

"Ben, you know that isn't fair!" she snapped. "I wanted to see how you were! Can't a mother do that? And I pay the rent for this place, I don't see why I can't–"

Byron stepped forward slightly, which forced the bodyguards to mirror his movements. He stopped and seemed to deflate, his shoulders curling in as he turned his eyes to the floor.

"You pay *half* the rent, which I never asked you to do," he muttered. Though he started quietly, an angry kind of despair seeped back in with every word. "You offered to pay it so you'd know where I was, well, you know where I've been for the last two weeks and you never bothered to visit. Now you walk in here unannounced, search my boyfriend's stuff without permission, and start an argument? No amount of money is worth that shit. So, feel free to stop paying, and leave."

"Ben, be reasonable, you know–"

"What do I know, mommy? Hmm? That I don't matter enough for you to take a twenty-minute drive from the office?"

"Stop being a child!"

The way Byron said 'mommy' had the bile rising in Ronan's throat. He'd sounded so completely broken, so absolutely worn down, and here was Byron's own mother shouting at him for it?

He refused to put up with any more of this. Ignoring the bodyguards, Ronan put himself between Byron and Gianna, one hand behind him to keep a grip on Byron's trembling arm.

"Mrs Williams," he said with a calm he didn't feel. "Please. Leave. You needn't worry about the rent; I'll cover whatever is necessary while I'm living here. Your son's medical decisions are his own to make. If – once he's had some space – he wants to see you or your husband, we will arrange that. Whatever your history, he's been through a traumatic experience and showing up here with armed men is not helping. So, please – leave. Now."

Gianna drew herself up to her full height – which was still significantly shorter than either Ronan or Byron – but her phone rang before she could speak. Her response was like a light switch. She immediately turned away from them and answered the call in a much more cheerful tone of voice.

She left without acknowledging them in the slightest. One of her bodyguards followed suit, while the other gave them an apologetic grimace on his way out.

"Well, that was fucked up," Ronan muttered, mostly to himself as he crossed the room to put the chain on the door. Standing rigidly still for so long had made his already sleep-stiffened knees seize up even further, and now every step felt like fire. "Urgh, I think I need to go back to bed after that."

Byron didn't reply.

At first when Ronan turned around again, he thought Byron had left the room – it was only when he sobbed out loud that he realized Byron was sitting on the floor with his back against the cabinets.

Ronan had never been fantastic with tears – his was a career that usually valued repressing rather than showing emotions – and coming from Byron he had no idea how to help him.

It wasn't just that Byron was a big, muscular guy – it was more the fact that Byron had approached almost everything since they met with either humor or anger. Seeing him brought to tears by his own mother was a horribly uncomfortable sight.

His first instinct was to sit on the floor beside him and give him a hug.

He'd barely been able to walk to the door though – if he got onto the floor, he'd never get up again. The living room was still wrecked so sitting on the couch was out of the question.

Ronan braced himself against the kitchen counter and held out his other hand.

"Come on," he said gently, "we're gonna go back to bed."

Byron looked up at him, but didn't take his hand. He clearly hadn't taken his eyeliner off the night before, and now it was running down his face. He looked like a cyberpunk raccoon.

Ronan must have had thought that last comment too loudly – Byron snorted through his tears, and tried to wipe the mess away. All he managed to achieve was a more comprehensive smear of kohl. He looked a mess.

Now that Ronan thought about it, they could probably both do with a wash. Hospital showers were always terrible and being clean might give Byron a fresh outlook on the situation. Plus, a bath together would give Ronan a chance to give Byron some physical comfort.

"Do you think your bathtub would fit two people?" Ronan asked.

"That thing won't even fit me," Byron shook his head, then added thoughtfully, "the shower will though."

"Good. Come on."

"I don't want you to think I'm vain–"

"Oh, don't worry. I've shared a bathroom with you for long enough to know that you're vain. Most people don't spend that many hours on their hair."

Byron just stared at him, the shower water slowly plastering locks of said hair across his forehead.

"Sorry," Ronan said at last. "I shouldn't have interrupted. Go on."

"Does my face bother you?"

To be honest, he'd never considered the question. Objectively speaking Byron's scars were quite extensive, but Ronan had been more focused on his own recovery – and the 'werewolf' question – to really think about it.

Ronan leaned back against the cold tiles to get a good look at the wall of man standing before him. There was a lot to look at, and in his opinion all of it was good.

Still, he took his time to study every inch, from the toenails that still bore traces of purple polish, to the top of his head where his roots were beginning to show more clearly.

All in all, he was a damn fine specimen of a man – even after weeks in the hospital with minimal exercise he had a physique to be envied, and while tattoos weren't everyone's cup of tea, Ronan found they highlighted rather than distracted from his looks.

He let his eyes drift down again.

Even if Byron lost the muscles entirely, he was very well hung – a hand blocked his view of that particular attribute.

"I asked about my face," Byron reminded him quietly.

Ronan shrugged, shivering a little when the gesture brought his skin into contact with colder tiles.

"I've always thought of you as a package deal," he explained, "You're not one good feature, you're a lot of very nice features all rolled together with some strangeness."

Byron sighed and tipped his head back. He looked like he was seconds away from stamping his foot in a full-on pout. Ronan hoped he wouldn't, the tile would be slippery and he didn't want to have to haul a man that size up off the floor all by himself.

"Look, I thought you were a beautiful prick when your face was 50% bandages–"

"Bandages are just...nothing! Anything could be underneath bandages!" Byron jabbed an angry finger towards his own cheek. "You had no idea I'd look like this!"

"For fuck's sake, I don't care!" Ronan shouted back. He could have gone on but as soon as the words came out of his mouth, he knew they'd been a mistake. Instead he took a deep breath and tried to speak more calmly. "Yes, I didn't know what was under there but frankly it doesn't matter. A few weeks ago, I was laid out dying in a desert trying not to look at my own legs splashed across the fucking landscape! A few scratches and burns absolutely do not matter to me. I've seen worse."

"What?"

Byron was peering down at Ronan's legs, leaning forward out of the shower's spray to get a better look.

The two long vertical incisions were still early in their healing process, the new pink scar tissue made redder by the warmth of the water and Ronan's agitation. The rest – smaller burns and surface shrapnel wounds – were starting to fade a little now. Once his leg hair grew back half of them wouldn't be visible at all any more.

"Not to call you a liar or anything, but those are definitely your legs. You'd have, like, seams or something if they weren't."

For a second or two Ronan considered bringing up one of his memories of that moment so Byron could see for himself, but he wasn't actually sure if his mind reading worked like that. Frankly he didn't want to face that trauma again right now.

"It's a long story. Or a weird one. I don't..." He sighed.

"Okay."

"What?"

"You don't have to talk about it."

"Are you in my head again?"

Byron rolled his eyes. "You can't shout things and then complain when people hear you."

Deciding to change the subject back to their original focus, Ronan stepped forward, reaching out for Byron's shoulders as he moved into the shower's spray again. He hadn't realized how cold he'd been getting at the far end of the cubicle until his hands touched Byron's skin.

He was so warm.

"How about you listen to me now?" Ronan said as he let his thumb trace over the shape of the scars that cut through Byron's shoulder tattoo. "You're fucking gorgeous. Scars are just reminders of being alive, and they will absolutely never bother me. But if they bother you, I will support you in any work that you want to get done. Hell, you're in eyeliner every day – you want to add foundation to that, I'm not going to complain so long as it doesn't come off on my clothes. But that's up to you."

He moved forward again, bringing their hips and chests together so he could press a gentle kiss to Byron's jaw where the scar had healed to leave a clear indent in the flesh.

"If you want to keep them uncovered it makes no difference to me." He kissed him again, following the line of the central deepest scar. "You're covered in strange tattoos, and you seem to be allergic to wearing a shirt – you chose those tattoos and I'm not going to make you hide them, so why would I make you hide something that you couldn't choose?"

Byron gave a rumbling sort of sigh, so deep in his chest that Ronan could swear he felt it through his solar plexus. He added another kiss in the hope of hearing it again.

"You're sure?" Byron asked instead. His hands had come up to wrap around Ronan's back, but they were hovering a millimeter or two from his skin, as if Byron didn't dare to complete the connection.

"Well," Ronan leaned back far enough to make eye contact and grinned. "I might ask you to cover up that gremlin on your stomach, or maybe add some sunglasses to it. I'm not a fan of being watched while I work."

That got him a snort of amusement, and Byron's hands finally closed the gap to hold him close. Content that he finally had his point across, Ronan let himself relax into the embrace, resting his head on Byron's uninjured shoulder and letting his arms drape over his back.

He could have stayed there all day, not doing anything but enjoying the comfort that came with being together. A year ago Ronan wouldn't have seen himself doing this – not just because of the rarity of private moments, but more from a simple disinterest in romantic moments. He couldn't remember the last time he'd had a boyfriend he just wanted to cuddle.

Of course, they were living together and sharing a bed – they could indulge in whatever they wanted, whenever they liked. There wasn't the urgency to steal time together. Their time was their own.

Byron turned his head slightly so that Ronan could feel his breath against his wet hair, but he didn't say anything. He just breathed, slowly and calmly until Ronan felt he could almost fall asleep there.

Unluckily for them both, that was the moment the hot water chose to run out.

"Pink or green?"

Ronan looked up from staring at his toes – he still couldn't comfortably bend his knees enough to dry his own feet, so he had been debating asking Byron to do it for him. He knew it was a normal part of recovery, but it was hard not to feel helpless and a bit embarrassed. He wasn't an old man yet.

"What?" he asked.

He hadn't really been listening to Byron while he stood fussing in front of the mirror and now, he didn't know what he was being asked about. Part of his brain presented him with the image of painted toenails, which definitely wasn't something he wanted.

"Pink or green?" Byron asked again, this time he lifted up a bleached strand of hair from the side of his head. "I need to dye my roots, and you wanted to go clothes shopping, I figured I might as well pick up a color while we're there."

"Oh, uh..."

Ronan had never really understood the urge to dye hair unusual colors – he'd had enough teasing about his own reddish hair as a child that he'd often wished for a less conspicuous brown. Thanks to many postings in sunny places his hair had naturally faded to a pale strawberry-blond for the last few years, and it was only now that his beard was growing in that he had to get used to the orange tones again.

"Umm..."

"Never mind," Byron said.

A quarter floated up from a dish full of pocket detritus and flipped itself to land on the dresser with a clink.

"Tails." Byron nodded happily to himself. "Green it is then."

That sort of thing might take some getting used to.

"Aren't you going to try anything on?" Byron asked from behind a bundle of clothes as Ronan led them towards the nearest cash register.

He bit back his first reply, which he knew would be far too grumpy for public consumption.

His knees were on fire.

No, that was the wrong word, he told himself as a vision of a dark desert flashed across his mind. Not on fire. Just in pain. Very, very intense pain.

It was safe to say that he hadn't really appreciated how good his medication was until he'd forgotten to take it. They'd given him the slow release stuff, so while he'd been uncomfortable when he woke, there'd still been some lingering benefits. Now, after a long cab ride and nearly an hour wandering around the mall, he was fully experiencing his pain for the first time.

The sensation wasn't just in his knees – they'd had to run pins into the femur and tibia of both legs. Perhaps it was just in his head but he could swear that he could feel where the metal ended inside the bones. Once he'd become aware of it, he found it impossible to ignore.

Why wasn't he trying anything on? He didn't think he could safely change his trousers right now. He was barely managing to walk in a straight line with both crutches. He'd fall, or get tangled up, or just end up screaming in the dressing room from the pain that was still building.

"It's all right, I know my size," he lied, as cheerfully as he could fake around gritted teeth. He didn't sound convincing.

They should not have come out. He should have just bought everything online, or spent a few more weeks lounging around Byron's apartment in borrowed clothes. It wasn't as if he had anywhere to be these days.

That thought depressed him almost as much as the pain.

He'd felt like he was making so much progress in physiotherapy and pottering around the hospital grounds. It had all been an illusion brought on by good medication.

He wasn't nearly as well as he'd thought.

It would take months for his new knees to fully settle, and he had nothing concrete to look forward to – other than spending more time with Byron, but that wasn't the same.

He'd had a career.

He'd had a future.

"But how do you know if it'll look good?" Byron had caught up with him, but didn't seem to be able to see him properly behind the clothes Ronan had picked out. For a moment Ronan worried that he might have overloaded him – Byron was injured too, after all – but he soon noticed that his right hand wasn't actually in contact with the pile. Whether he was holding it all with telekinesis or was carrying most of the weight on the left Ronan couldn't tell.

Well, Byron was a big boy, if it was a problem, he'd just have to raise it himself.

"What do you mean 'look good'?" Ronan asked, trying not to sound facetious.

He'd mostly picked out t-shirts and cargo pants, with a few button ups thrown in. Soft pajamas. Underwear – various. The only thing he'd really thought about for more than a few seconds were socks. Good boots were the key to a good life but poor-quality socks would let you down every time.

"This is all...brown." Byron pronounced the word as if it was somehow offensive to him.

"Not really, there's tan and russet and beige and um–"

"Brown, brown, and brown. Ronan, seen at a distance this looks a lot like camo."

There wasn't anything he could really say to that. He hadn't actually picked anything that was camouflage print, but seen as one big pile, Byron did have a point.

"Look," he said at last. "I've been in some kind of uniform since I was five. I know what size I wear, and I picked those sizes. I know what the clothes will look like – they will look like a covering for my body, which currently wants to lay down on the floor right now because I forgot my meds, so if we could just buy this and go–"

"Oh, no, I didn't realize!" Byron said.

He shuffled forward in what looked like it would be an attempt at a hug, but Ronan headed on towards the cash register before the whole pile of clothes ended up on the floor. Or he ended up there himself.

"Why didn't you say something before we set off?"

"Byron, if I'd remembered that I'd forgotten them before we set off, I wouldn't have forgotten them."

That just got him a funny look. Apparently, logic wasn't Byron's strong suit, but also Ronan knew he shouldn't have been so snippy with him. He was coming from a place of concern after all.

"Do you really never try anything on?" Byron asked again once they were sitting in the half-empty food court. He'd insisted on getting them both iced coffees and had all but forced Ronan into a chair.

Ronan would have preferred to have gone straight home, but Byron still had things he wanted to pick up, and he had to admit that sitting was a relief.

A woman walked by with fluffy grey cat ears poking out from among unnaturally blue curls.

"Don't worry, she's just into anime," Byron added when he saw Ronan following her movements.

"Yes, I know, I can tell when it's a costume, thank you. Just a bit odd to see in a shopping centre, that's all," he said with a shrug. "And no, I don't try anything on. Outside of getting fitted for dress uniforms and formal suits. I don't see the point. I'm a tall, skinny guy, I buy clothes for tall, skinny guys."

"But that's my point, you could wear anything and look amazing. Did you really not experiment when you were younger?" Byron was twisting his fingers through his hair, pulling the locks so they hung away from the shaved side of his head. Ronan couldn't tell if it was a habitual gesture or if Byron was getting anxious about his hair being a boring color. He did seem to be trying to hide the natural brown.

"When I came back from school for the summer it didn't seem like a good use of my time. I'd just grab whatever looked like it would fit from the nearest, cheapest shop. Now I buy quality because it lasts so much longer, but I can't say I care."

Byron was looking at him like he'd personally insulted every religious icon Byron had ever worshipped.

In a way he probably had.

"I'm going to buy you so many things."

"No thank you."

"I'm gonna," Byron said.

Before Ronan could protest any further Byron had slapped the table, pointed at him in a resolute fashion, and already started to walk away.

"Look, just get me something useful – like paracetamol!" he called after him.

Byron waved but Ronan couldn't tell if he'd actually heard him.

Without any other options – he didn't feel like walking any further, and he couldn't remember the address to head home – Ronan settled back in his chair and stared at the ceiling.

While the sitting had reduced the pain in his legs a little, it wasn't enough. He wanted to prop them up on the empty chair opposite, but he had the sneaking suspicion that if he got his feet up there, he wouldn't be able to get them back down again on his own.

He'd asked the ifrit to fix him.

This didn't feel like being fixed.

There was more to what he'd told Byron than just a simple lack of interest in his appearance.

True, he'd never really cared about what he wore. When he was younger, he could have worn a bin bag and still been attractive to the kind of guy who valued delicate good looks. There had been a few summers where he'd never needed to pay for anything, where every bar had someone – many someones – who were willing to cover his tab for five minutes of his attention.

He'd never really connected with any of those people. While there might be a little affection there from time to time, he'd known he was using them as a means to an end, whether the end was a drink or a warm bed.

The others, the ones who weren't human, he'd felt better able to relate to at first.

He was a human who knew there was more to the world than what humans saw – they *were* the more. He could talk to them in ways he could never talk to the average person. Over the years it had started to feel hollow, and almost fetishistic, to be always seeking out beings just for their differences. That wasn't fair to them.

Not that there weren't creatures who were just as obsessed with humanity as he was with non-humans – vampires, for example. He'd never met a vampire that didn't love to be around humans, it probably let them relive a little something of what they'd lost.

Still, whoever it was that he found, it never worked out. The connections were always superficial, not built to last. Bad things had happened, more than once, and in a way that he could never really talk to anyone about. Relationships of any kind had become too much to bear.

The army had been a good excuse to avoid dealing with the issue – if he was always moving, always away, well, who could blame him for not committing to anything long term?

Something about Byron felt different. Ronan had been drawn to him from the first moment he saw him, long before he realized he was more than superficially odd.

Or was that feeling simply an effect of Ronan's situation – was he trapped here, or did he genuinely want to stay?

As he stared at the floor his thoughts were derailed by a sudden sensation of being watched.

Someone was standing silently, three feet to his left. He hadn't noticed their arrival.

On first impression he wondered if he'd been thinking too loudly again, because this person looked like the textbook definition of a vampire, if that textbook had been written by someone with very little imagination.

There was lace. There was velvet. There were fishnet stockings worn on both legs *and* arms. There was even a widow's peak haircut and fangs. The image would have been perfect if the fangs hadn't been a different color than the rest of their teeth. Ronan suspected they probably glowed in the dark.

"Can I help you?" he asked, when it became clear that this person wasn't going to say anything.

"You've bought a lot of things."

Their voice would have been creepy in its low monotonous tone if it weren't for the strong Appalachian accent.

Ronan tried not to laugh. "Yes. This is a shopping mall."

"Are you Byron's daddy?"

Thankfully for Ronan's continued ability to ever be seen in public again, he managed to bite back his instinctive reply that 'of course he wasn't Byron's father.' If that had actually come out of his mouth he would have literally died of embarrassment.

Instead he was only partially dying at the implication that he was Byron's sugar daddy.

Usually, that dynamic was about age and status, but, financially speaking, he suspected Byron was actually better off than he was – at least until Ronan's grandfather finally accepted his own death and let him inherit.

"I don't think he needs a sugar daddy," Ronan said as casually as he could.

The strange person in front of him nodded thoughtfully and rubbed at their neck.

Where Ronan would have expected to see some kind of melodramatic bite marks there were just a series of horizontal lines. He couldn't tell if the lines were tattoos or scarification and, frankly, it wasn't his business.

"What happened to his face?" the newcomer went on.

"Who are you?"

A pale hand pointed towards an alternative-looking shop. It seemed to be filled with dragon figurines and plastic skulls, but it was hard to tell through the thick cloud of what Ronan hoped was incense. If it wasn't incense, then the building was on fire.

"I work there." Not the best answer but probably all Ronan was going to get.

For a moment he was distracted by the glimmer of their skin. They had so much body glitter on their hands it almost looked like fish scales.

"We hadn't seen him for a while. We were worried. I didn't get a chance to ask him, when he came in earlier. Usually he stays a while. We figured he had someone new. Damien saw him with you, so..." They trailed off like this speech was the verbal equivalent of running a marathon.

Of course there was someone called Damien working in a shop like that.

The newcomer coughed into their hand, a dry uncomfortable sound that reminded Ronan of his first few days in the desert, when hydration had a steep learning curve. He almost instinctively offered them a drink, then decided against it, just in case they really were a vampire.

"There was an accident, but he'll be fine," he said. Byron's story was his own to tell, and there was no way in hell Ronan was going to tell anyone his boyfriend got hurt playing with a flaming sword. He'd rather be mistaken for his sugar daddy than admit to that.

"Cool." Their voice was barely a whisper, and Ronan felt more than a little bad when they moved their hand away from their face. He hadn't noticed before but their lips were terribly dry. "Well, tell him Melusine said hi."

"I will," he said, but they were already drifting back towards their store.

He'd almost finished his coffee when he finally remembered where he recognized that name from. He had no concrete evidence – they could have just been the sort of goth who named themselves after a river spirit and was bad at staying hydrated – but if the cloud around their shop was vapor rather than smoke...

He should make some notes.

Ronan wasn't going to go interrogate anyone – Byron probably knew about them anyway, like he'd known about the delivery guy – but it was still an interesting thing to have encountered. One kind of supernatural entity dressing as another.

He hadn't brought a notepad, but the back of a receipt would do for now.

The couch was the most comfortable thing he'd ever encountered in his entire life.

He was never going to leave it again.

Ronan sighed and stretched, wriggling further down into the embrace of the cushions beneath him. Thank all the gods and the pharmaceutical industry for the gift that was decent pain medication.

On the subject of gifts, he was also grateful for the warmth of the other new clothes Byron had buried him under as soon as they made it home. Apparently, Byron was working on the basis that Ronan couldn't turn down gifts he couldn't physically escape from, though to Ronan's surprise his choices hadn't been nearly as garish as expected.

In protest of Ronan's usual palette of browns, Byron had brought him a selection of t-shirts in shades of blue-green, several pairs of jeans with price tags Byron had pre-emptively removed, and a green knitted sweater that would probably make Ronan look like a very sophisticated leprechaun.

Although he didn't have the energy – or flexibility – to try anything on just yet, he already knew the clothes would be a perfect fit. Everything was impossibly soft, and simplistic in a way that suggested expense rather than frugality. He didn't want to imagine how much it had all cost.

Ronan had tried to carefully hint that Byron was being too generous, and perhaps some of the items should be returned, but Byron had responded to that suggestion by eating the receipt.

Not exactly the most mature response, but entirely in character.

Well, he knew all about picking his battles and not looking gift horses in the mouth, so Ronan wasn't going to argue any further.

He might need some persuading to wear the green sweater in public though.

At least it would match with Byron's hair.

He watched as Byron pottered around the apartment in nothing but his underwear. It was a good view. He said he always did this while dyeing his hair – it wasn't possible to get stains on clothes you weren't wearing and sitting around in the bathroom was a waste of time.

So far that was the only thing about Byron's behavior that made sense. Watching him wander around was like watching a bumblebee in an overgrown flower bed – a lot seemed to be happening with very little rhyme or reason.

A sock was retrieved from the floor and thrown into the hamper, but not the shirt that was a few centimeters to the left of it. Items were removed from bags one at a time despite all their contents ultimately going in the same direction.

There was no order to what he was doing, and if his arse hadn't looked as good as it did in teal underpants Ronan would have had to look away out of frustration.

To distract himself from the madness he said, "A friend of yours said 'hello' by the way, someone called Melusine?"

Byron paused in the act of straightening half a stack of magazines.

As he frowned Ronan couldn't help noticing that he was dyeing his eyebrows as well.

"Mellow-scene," he said slowly, "Melo – oh, from the homewares place?"

"Maybe? All I could see through the pall of smoke was skulls and bats. I wouldn't really call those décor items."

"No?" Byron grinned and crossed the apartment in a few strides to reach behind the couch. "You won't like Eddie then."

"I'm not sure I want – oh. That's a skeleton." It was wearing a party hat. "Why do you have a life-sized skeleton?"

Byron was holding the thing by its neck with one hand. With the other he made it wave.

Ronan wondered once more why he found Byron so attractive.

"The important question is 'why not?' Sometimes he sits out on the balcony," Byron said, as if his words were entirely logical. "But, yeah, I got him at Melusine's place a while ago. The mist is from essential oil vaporizers or something, it's not smoke."

"Not to be rude but are they...human?" Damn. There really was no subtle way to ask that question. "That you know of?" he added, in the hope that the extra words might improve things. They didn't.

Without looking at him again Byron dropped Eddie with a clatter, grabbed the old takeout containers from the table, and headed back towards the kitchen.

"Do you think everyone I know is a monster?"

"No, I wouldn't use that word. They were clearly a person, but a person doesn't have to be human. Like your other friend, uh..." Just his luck that his medication would decide to start affecting his brain just when he didn't want to seem like a total dick. "Donnie, that was his name. Trust me, I've known non-human people myself, and Melusine *does* have the same name as a river spirit. They were very dehydrated. Plus, they seemed to have scales, and, you know, gills."

The silence that followed was occasionally broken by the sounds of objects being jammed into a dishwasher.

Ronan couldn't see Byron from where he was laying, and he really didn't want to stand up right now. It seemed he'd become used to the effects of his medication with constant use and missing a dose for thirty-six hours had made them feel more potent.

"Look, I'm sorry, I was curious–"

"You keep making nebulous references to other creatures, but you've never actually told me how you've known them," Byron said. It was hard to gauge his mood without reading his expression, but Ronan would have guessed at 'unhappy.' "You weren't all that surprised by a shapeshifter attacking us in the hospital, but you freaked out about a guy delivering take out, so..."

Byron trailed off without finishing his point.

What had he called Ronan before? Speciesist?

That was hardly fair.

It was probably a bad idea to go for shock value, but Ronan was annoyed, and starting to feel like he was floating in a nauseating kind of way, so he opted for honesty.

"Do you want a complete list of everyone I've ever met, or just the ones I slept with? I mean, the second list is about seventy percent of the first, but–"

Byron reappeared like a jack springing out of its box, with a mug in each hand and a mildly horrified look on his face.

"You *slept* with them?"

Ronan shrugged and turned his eyes towards the ceiling. "Now who's being speciesist?"

He felt quite smug about that line until he remembered what Byron had told him about his own first boyfriend. "Wait, didn't you say you slept with a warlock?"

"Yeah, but warlocks are human."

"Debatable."

"Okay, fine, he was, like, two thousand years old," Byron said.

Ronan hadn't heard him cross the room but he felt the warmth against his arm when Byron sat on the floor with his back against the couch.

"Sorry," he went on, "I shouldn't judge."

"Neither of us should."

"You can't just start talking about sleeping with non-humans and just end it there you know," Byron prompted when the companionable silence had dragged on longer than his curiosity could possibly endure. Which was about eighty-five seconds.

"Okay. I'm not telling you everything – because I'm tired, and a man needs his mysteries sometimes – but how about I tell you about the first one I slept with, and the last one I met?"

Beside him Byron shuffled around so he could lean his elbow on the couch and stare at Ronan's face. It was a bit more intimate than he might like for this conversation but at least he got a good view of an impressive bicep.

"So, first few weeks at the academy I met this guy called Tristan. A bit shorter than me, about as pale, not sure on his age but says he's got a degree in botany or something. Really sweet, funny, great kisser, and he's really into doing stuff for me. But anytime I try to touch below the belt it's a no go. Which is a big issue because – I know people have preferences – but I like to reciprocate. It's most of the fun for me."

"Did he have, like, tentacles down there?" Byron asked with a grimace. "Cloaca? Teeth?"

"Am I telling this story or not?"

"Sorry."

"Anyway," Ronan continued, "he also had this thing about never having his mouth on me for very long and I'm getting really self-conscious, you know, like – is it me? Is he actually even gay? Is he a virgin and he's too shy to admit it? So, I have to sit him down and have this really awkward 'I like you but I don't think we're sexually compatible' conversation, which at nineteen was the most cringe-inducing conversation I'd ever had to have with a person."

Even sixteen years later he could still feel his shoulders tightening just at the thought of how horribly it had gone.

"And?"

"He started crying."

"Oh my god."

"Yeah! But then, he finally manages to say that he really liked me too, but he's got this medical condition that basically means he's got erectile dysfunction. Which was the last thing I would have thought of, because, you know, he's young, but it certainly is not a deal breaker for me. Normal human problem, I'm adaptable, there are things that can help. I say we can look into getting toys and stuff together."

Much to Ronan's relief Byron was nodding through most of what he was saying. They'd been open with each other so far, but there was always that risk that a new partner would get strange about old ones.

Since Byron seemed to be okay Ronan went on. "We got some things, he's all psyched up and then he admits that the reason for his oral issue is that he likes to bite. And he finds it hard to resist the temptation. Again, that doesn't bother me, I'll try anything once. Half an hour later we've gotten over-excited, and..."

He trailed off, not entirely sure how to phrase the next part.

"Did he actually bite you?" Byron prompted. "Or transform into something?"

"No, he slid it in and it's like a block of ice." He shivered at that particular memory. "And, weirdly – despite dating this guy for an entire month – this was the moment when I noticed he didn't actually have a heartbeat. Or breathe, except when he was talking."

"What?"

"He was a fucking vampire."

Byron snorted. "Literally. Did you really not notice the whole 'not going out in daylight, lack of reflection' thing?"

"Nope, because that's not actually true. I mean he was a bit lethargic during the day but how would you even notice that – everyone's tired at the academy."

"So, how did you get away from him?"

Ronan's medication really must have reached its peak because he didn't understand the question at all.

"You said you were having sex when you realized," Byron said slowly, like Ronan was some kind of idiot. "So, did you just make your excuses or stake him or what?"

He shook his head. He still didn't get it.

Byron sighed. "How. Did. You. Escape. The. Vampire?"

Every word was punctuated by a tap on Ronan's chest, not in a threatening way, but clearly an attempt to get Ronan's attention.

"Ooooh. I didn't," Ronan said when the light finally dawned. "He was really good in bed. We dated until mid-December. We just decided he wouldn't do oral since I wasn't interested in immortality or anemia."

Even after all this time – and finding a guy as great as Byron – the way it all ended still made him a little melancholy. "Then he found this cute medic who was willing to be bitten and, you know, it wasn't fair for me to ask him to give up the chance to drink something other than livestock blood for the first time in years. So, I let him go. I think they both work in a blood bank in Estonia now."

"Aww, well, that's sweet in a really fucked up way, I guess," Byron chuckled.

Ronan stretched, hoping that a change in position might wake his brain up a bit, but the movement just made him yawn.

"Urgh, I need to go to bed. Care to join me?"

"Are you sure you wouldn't prefer someone a bit colder?" Byron teased, though he tempered his words by pressing a kiss to Ronan's forehead.

"No, I'm very happy with my relationship with a red-hot, bed-hogging octopus man."

"Hey!" This time Byron laughed outright. It was quickly becoming Ronan's favorite sound.

Ronan was only halfway through asking for a hand getting up by the time Byron had grabbed him and started carrying him bridal-style towards the bedroom.

"When did this become a 'relationship'?" Byron asked under the cover of darkness.

They hadn't been in bed more than five minutes, Ronan laid on his side and Byron wrapped tight around his back, but clearly this was a question that couldn't wait until morning.

"I don't know." That was the honest truth.

Ronan swallowed and wondered how much else to say. Well, what did he have to lose by laying it all out? Nothing at all.

"I, uh, I told your mother this was my home, and I think I called you my boyfriend, too. I guess it just...it seems right. Does that both–"

"No." Byron cut him off before he could finish the question. "No, it doesn't bother me. I'm pretty sure I said the same. Thank you, for what you said to Gianna. And for staying."

"Hey, I like it here."

He smiled as Byron's lips brushed against his neck, then realizing that Byron couldn't see his face he reached down and wove their fingers together.

He was almost asleep when Byron said, "You never told me about the last creature you met."

"I met someone in the desert. He was made of fire." It all seemed like a dream right now. "He gave me my legs back. They were...Byron, believe me when I say they were *gone*. There's no surgery in the world that could have repaired what happened. I think he's the reason I'm here. There's absolutely no other explanation – I should not have woken up in a hospital halfway around the world."

"Hmmm. Spooky," Byron mumbled against his hair.

"Doesn't that worry you, though? I've been trying not to think about it but–"

"I'm not worried. If something else weird happens, we'll deal with it."

Ronan nodded. Sleep was just too close to focus on anything right now. Byron was right – they could manage whatever happened next.

That night he dreamed of an empty desert, endless stars, and a deep voice pointing out which constellations looked vaguely obscene. Whether Byron had actually wandered into his head, or his imagination had just presented him with that image, Ronan decided he'd rather not know.

9

Time moves strangely during recovery. Weeks passed in a blur of intense physical therapy interspersed with periods of such bone-deep exhaustion that Ronan barely noticed how little he was actually doing outside of his doctors' offices.

When he wasn't in a hydrotherapy pool, or being supervised in the gym, or slowly walking around the park opposite their apartment, Ronan spent most of his days half-asleep on the couch.

He'd listened to everything his doctors originally told him. He'd understood that after surgery like his it could take six weeks or more to walk without crutches, but he'd made the mistake of thinking that would mean he would be healed by then.

He was a fit, healthy man in his mid-thirties. Even though he'd medically discharged from the army, he'd believed that he would bounce back. Life was never that simple.

Byron had tried to help, but their injuries were very different. Within a week of being released from the hospital Byron was back to running ten miles or more a day, and had soon adapted his intimidatingly complex exercise routine to protect his injured shoulder.

Ronan had never seen someone doing a thousand sit-ups for fun before. There was always an excellent view involved, but even watching him made Ronan feel tired.

Much to his credit Byron was always willing to join Ronan in bed when he gave up on the couch, and to offer a variety of reasons to stay in bed for as long as possible. While recovery was slow, they were both men of flexible imaginations – it didn't take them long to find ways around their physical limitations to get off together at least twice a night.

Ronan might be tired, but he wasn't dead yet.

There was no way he'd let the chance of sharing a bed with a man like Byron go to waste.

He'd never lived with another person like this. He'd never had a partner at his fingertips all day, with little else to occupy his time. There were plenty of things they could do that didn't take up too much energy, and the things that did Ronan was happy to count towards his daily activity targets.

Plus, pleasure was a great distraction from the pain.

When they weren't sleeping, or exercising, or otherwise physically engaged, they talked. About everything and nothing. Movies they liked, songs they had in common, books, food, travel, family. Ronan had never expected to open up to anyone about that last topic.

He'd always been wary of telling anyone about the strange encounters of his childhood, but Byron listened with interest and the occasional joke. Where Byron came from money, Ronan had come from lost prestige – his grandfather had a title, and a genuinely haunted manor house, but barely a penny to his name. His mother had been written out of the will when she disappeared on a journey of self-discovery when he was ten and never came back. His father treated him more like an investment than a thing to be nurtured. They barely spoke and his life was all the better for that.

Ultimately Ronan's upbringing hadn't been ideal, but his family hadn't really shaped him.

On the other hand, Byron seemed barely able to escape the influence of his family, even when they weren't there. Although it was never entirely clear why that was the case.

His father was distant. His mother wanted to be involved but never found the time. There were mentions of an uncle and his partner, and of course Darcey, his only cousin; but so much seemed to be left unsaid. Ronan could feel holes in every narrative. When Byron spoke about his inability to refuse his mother anything – and his unending, soul-stunting fear of disappointing her again – it was never clear how he'd disappointed her in the first place.

Byron would skirt around certain topics – mentioning stays in various behavioral camps, military schools, boarding school, even a stint spent in a facility overseas – but he'd never explain the reasons. Occasionally a word would slip out, framing some specific incident in a way that sparked concern without adding any particular context.

Ronan could deal with a lot, but veiled references to 'The Fire' made him wonder exactly what he'd gotten into and how best to make it work.

If Gianna hadn't just let herself into the apartment, he might have been less concerned about managing Byron's relationship with his family. Whether Mac was supposed to keep an eye on Byron after the hospital or not, they'd seen no signs of anyone spying on them.

Still, people being able to walk straight into his home without permission wasn't something Ronan was willing to put up with – he'd had enough of dormitories for a lifetime. He wanted some privacy, and the chance for his boyfriend to heal.

They'd had such great plans, but never the energy to actually execute any of them.

The various quotations from locksmiths for changing the locks, and adding security measures, had been on the fridge door for weeks. The fridge that Ronan was currently peering into in search of eggs and bacon.

It was a Monday morning, he'd had all weekend to rest, his legs felt better than they had in a long time, he'd just made love to Byron in the shower, and now he was going to cook him breakfast as a surprise.

He should have learned his lesson from Gianna walking in all those weeks ago. He should have put the chain on the door. He should have put on some clothes. He shouldn't have been singing along with the radio quite so loudly.

But, sadly, 'should' is not the same as 'did'.

Which was why his first encounter with Darcey Vitale began with a scream.

The second time they met, ten minutes later – once Ronan was fully dressed, and Byron had retrieved his giggling cousin from the end of the hallway – she at least had the decency to offer to shake his hand.

Ronan had been about to apologize himself, for shouting something rude about Americans never locking doors or knocking before opening them, when she winked at him and said–

"Sorry for screaming at your penis. I'm sure it's very nice for people who are into that sort of thing. My cousin must be a lucky man."

Suddenly it didn't seem all that surprising that Byron had chosen to fight her with a flaming sword.

Since breakfast was inevitably ruined by the drama of her arrival, Darcey had insisted on taking them both to her favorite barbecue place on the promise of strong coffee and huge plates of meat.

That promise would have been more appealing if it hadn't also been followed by a penis joke.

Even though she was the perky polar-opposite to her cousin, it was clear they shared a sense of humor.

Ronan hoped that the addition of caffeine to his bloodstream might make her easier to deal with – bubbly wasn't a personality type he was used to encountering up close.

Still, he knew he should try to get along with her, even if she had joined the growing list of Byron's family members who had seen more of his body that he would like. At this rate he dreaded to think what would happen when they finally met Byron's father – if Gianna had seen him in his underwear, and Darcey saw him naked, then David was probably going to walk in on them in bed together.

That was a horrible thought he never wanted to have again.

Despite her physical resemblance to her aunt, Darcey spoke to him with respect – warmth, even.

She began by apologizing for never making it to their hospital to visit. Although Byron had taken the brunt of the damage, Darcey had still suffered burns of her own during the accident.

"By the time I could stand to wear a shirt, you guys were already at home and I figured I'd let you enjoy the honeymoon period," she said, suggestively wiggling her eyebrows.

"What?" Maybe Ronan should ask the waitress to leave the coffee pot with him, because he was already struggling to follow the conversation. "What honeymoon?"

"Oh, I don't mean literally," Darcey laughed, "I just meant, you know, when someone moves in with their new partner it's only polite to give them some space to get to know each other. And break in all the furniture."

Ronan tried to give Byron a look, but he was too busy howling with laughter to notice.

"How did you know about me though?" he asked. Not that he wanted Byron to keep him a secret but, still, it felt strange to know they'd been talking about him.

To answer his question, she handed him her phone, open to a folder containing a frighteningly large number of picture messages that Byron sent her over the previous few weeks.

The first message had the caption 'OMG look @ this cutie' under a photograph of Ronan immediately post-surgery with a mass of tubes still down his throat. Which must have been taken two days prior to their first meeting, what with Ronan being unconscious for most of that time.

Byron merely shrugged at the side eye Ronan gave him, as if taking photos of your sleeping roommate without their knowledge was somehow a normal thing.

The pictures only slightly improved after that – in some of them he was actually awake, though he was rarely aware the pictures were being taken. Then again, he would never have expected anyone to take quite that many photographs of him.

He'd only read through half of them by the time the waitress came back to get their orders.

The restaurant seemed to pride itself on serving street food in a gourmet – and therefore more expensive – presentation. They'd ended up being seated by one of the star attractions of the open kitchen – a huge metal dish suspended on chains over open flames to cook the meat. Ronan had seen such things often enough in European winter markets. It was hardly state of the art, but the others seemed impressed so he kept his mouth shut.

Something about the constant flickering of the flames made the hair at the nape of his neck stand on end. In search of distraction he took to looking around the room while Byron negotiated for the largest plate of food the restaurant could provide.

A black woman was watching them from a table by the window. At first, he wasn't quite sure if she was looking at them or the kitchen, but her eyes followed Byron's hands one too many times to be a coincidence.

When Ronan gave her a little wave she looked away.

Another one of David's friends sent to spy on them? What would be the point of that? Byron did have his hair tied back, and the scarred side of his face turned towards her. It was much more likely that she was being rude rather than a spy.

"I had, uh, I kinda had an ulterior motive for visiting," Darcey said quietly, drawing Ronan's attention back to the group.

Across the table Byron nodded as if he'd been expecting that confession all along.

Ronan felt his shoulders tensing, but kept his mouth shut for now. It wasn't his place to interfere with their family life. Not yet anyway.

Food had appeared from somewhere. He reached for a fork.

"I mean, obviously I wanted to meet the infamous Ronan, and see how you were doing after, you know–" she made a gesture towards her face, indicating Byron's scar, "and I was all set to visit a few weeks ago, but Gianna said to give you some time."

The two men glanced at each other. Ronan couldn't begin to speculate on Gianna's reasoning; Byron made a grimace that said much the same.

"Anyway," Darcey tried to begin, but got no further. Instead she stared down at her own plate, her short curls covering her eyes in a very Byron-like posture.

Ronan wondered whether Byron's hair would turn that same caramel color if he stopped dyeing it long enough for the sun to lighten it.

Just when the silence seemed to be dragging out too long, she suddenly huffed out a sigh and shook her hair back. The smile that she gave as she glanced up seemed almost angry, if such a thing were possible.

"Anyway, now your mother *needed* me to come see you. Because both she and Dad have asked me to ask you to come to David's birthday at the house next weekend." Every word was pronounced like Darcey was personally offended by it. "It's his seventieth."

"No. It isn't," Byron said flatly. "He doesn't have a birth certificate. No one knows when he was born."

"It's as close as they could–"

"I don't want to."

Darcey reached across the table, almost knocking over a glass, and tried to grab his hand. Whether he meant to or not, Byron pulled away.

Darcey's smile became slightly more brittle.

"I know," she said gently, "and I wouldn't normally ask. I'm not their messenger. I understand that you and your father don't get along–"

Byron's hand came down on the table hard enough to make the cutlery jump.

"David is an asshole. You're not old enough to remember how bad things were."

"I remember more than you think!" Darcey snapped, half rising from her chair before she seemed to think better of the escalation. "I do remember. I don't understand what caused it all, and I wasn't old enough to do anything, but – I swear to you, I do remember. I know Gianna and David are always trying to smooth things over and pretend everything was all lovey-dovey all the time. I know it's all fake. I'm not asking for David; I'm asking for *me*."

"That makes no sense!"

Ronan managed to resist the urge to bang his head on the table but only because there wasn't space among the plates.

"Byron, listen," he said, knowing immediately that his tone sounded like he was talking to a pair of wayward Privates rather than people he actually liked. "Sorry, just, please listen. Darcey, why do you want Byron to go?"

She smiled gratefully at him.

"I was hoping I could talk you both into coming along. Because 'the cute guy Byron managed to pick up in a hospital while covered in bandages' would make a much more interesting and distracting guest than, uh," she blushed and grinned, "you know, 'the hot girl pilot that Darcey picked up when she was supposed to be detailing her dad's jet'."

If there was more to this story Ronan didn't get to hear it.

There was a crash from the kitchen area.

One of the chefs had slipped and seemed to fall in slow motion, arms outstretched, onto the suspended cooking surface.

The chains closest to the point of impact snapped under the weight, tipping the chef, and all the cooking meat, into the fire pit below.

There wasn't much delay between the initial crash and the man's colleagues leaping into action to rescue him, but in Ronan's mind it might as well have been a thousand years.

The screaming, the crackling of fat hitting the fire, and the smell of the burning meat had flicked mental switches that Ronan didn't know he had.

He was outside, sitting on the curb with his head between his knees, before he even realized he was moving.

He should have expected this, some calm inner monologue tried to tell him over the cacophonous panic of the rest of his brain. How many times had he taken courses on spotting trauma symptoms in his own troops? Why hadn't he sought out help in advance? Why had he been so stupid?

Ronan didn't really register the admonishments.

They were all just background noise.

He was too focused on trying to separate reality, memory, and fictional construct; and the fact that he knew two conflicting simultaneous realities was not helping.

He knew – deep in his bones and at the very core of his being – that he had lost his legs in Iraq.

He tried not to think about that too much.

Most days he was successful.

Ignoring that fact didn't make it untrue.

He was walking through his days on feet that he knew he shouldn't have; commanding muscles that had been reduced to torn ribbons; using nerves he'd felt burn away. He knew the smell of his own smoldering flesh, his own bones as they charred.

He had felt all of this as he'd laid there negotiating for his life with a being that shouldn't exist, and he still knew it now as the odor of the restaurant accident clung to the back of his throat.

Something was telling his senses that he was laid on his back bleeding to death in a cold desert wasteland.

Everything that had happened since – the hospital; the operations; the monster; the beautiful wonderful lunatic – all of that took on the consistency of mist and seemed to blow away from him, curling tendrils of thought that evaporated every time he tried to grab for them.

Giving up on memory, he tried to focus outwards instead.

He could feel the ground under him.

He could.

The pavement was sun-hot under his backside.

He wasn't wearing his full combat gear – he was wearing a t-shirt that pulled tight across his back and cargo pants that cut in around his hips.

He could feel the sun on his exposed arms and on the crown of his head.

He wasn't cold. He wasn't burning. It wasn't night time.

Ronan shifted, wrapping his arms around his legs and pressing his face against his knees. His knees that absolutely were there; his knees that ached where the deep scars were still healing around the replacement metal structures; his knees and lower legs that could sense the touch of his fingers and the warmth of his breath through his trousers; that were not on fire or blown to shreds; that were real; that were his, his, his–

A cool hand settled between his shoulder-blades. It was a soft, tentative touch from a hand much smaller than the one he'd been expecting.

"Can you hear me?"

The voice was feminine, but it wasn't Darcey.

Ronan tipped his head, keeping his cheek pressed against his knee.

It was the woman who'd been watching them in the restaurant.

Seen up close, she was one of those women who seemed perpetually on the edge of middle age, with a frosting of grey curls at her temples and more laughter lines than her earlier expression would have suggested.

Something about her bearing made him want to salute her, even if the coral suit she was wearing lacked any kind of military tailoring. It didn't need to when her posture said 'commanding officer in the room.'

He tried to sit up straighter, his body automatically trying to shift out of this informal slump, but her hand held him in place.

"I heard Ben tell your waitress that you were an injured veteran," she said. Her tone was blessedly no-nonsense. Ronan didn't think he could bear to be treated gently right now. "I suppose that happened recently, given your age?"

Ronan blinked slowly at her. Since he was first able to speak, he'd been taught how to address those who were his superiors, but with the fire still roaring at the edge of his consciousness it was hard to focus. All he had left was one solid marble of knowledge.

"His name is Byron, ma'am."

The woman smiled slightly. "I've known him since before he was born."

"Forgive me ma'am, I've known my father's best friend since he was just a Captain, but I'd never dream of addressing him by anything other than General. Just because you knew Byron before he changed his name..."

The woman laughed, a low melodious sound with a hint of the same cigarette gravel as Gianna. He wondered how they knew one another. Perhaps this was one of the people she'd been trying to impress when she'd been pushing Byron to play happy families as a child.

"Good point, young man. Good point." She leaned forward enough to offer him a handshake. "I apologize. And what rank should I address you with?"

"I'm retired, ma'am. I was a Major. Ronan Cox, Parachute Regiment." The last words had added themselves automatically to his name. Another sign that he hadn't come to terms with the change as much as he'd been pretending.

"Hello, Admiral Blake."

Hearing Byron's deep rumble was a relief that Ronan could only have described with the floweriest of poetic terms. How the hell had he fallen so hard, so fast?

Under the relief, a part of him instinctively panicked at having been insubordinate towards an Admiral – even though she was clearly a member of another country's armed forces and he was no longer a serving officer – but it was a small voice that was easily ignored once he'd shifted his head enough to look directly at Byron.

"Hello, Byron dear," she said, her smile growing when Byron's face showed clear confusion at the use of his legal name, "your friend here was just reminding me that it's polite to use people's proper form of address."

"In that case it would be more correct to call him my *boy*friend," Byron said, returning her smile with a grin before he turned his attention back to the man in question. "Are you okay, Ronan? Darcey's getting the food to go, we can take it home and eat there if you like?"

Ronan nodded.

He accepted the offered hand, but only for long enough to get upright and wrap an arm around Byron's torso. Right now, he needed something to ground him in the real world, and nothing was more grounding than that wall of muscle.

"Will I see you at David's birthday party?" she called after them as they headed towards where Darcey was waiting.

To Ronan's surprise, Byron nodded.

After a few steps Byron draped his own arm around Ronan's waist.

He couldn't tell if it was some kind of telekinesis or just adrenaline but Ronan felt lighter and moved easier despite only being able to use one crutch. He wondered whether his physiotherapist would approve that technique or if he was unknowingly hurting his recovery. He didn't care – he felt loved.

"We're really going to go to this birthday party? After everything you said about David? I thought you wanted to limit contact with your parents." Ronan tried to keep the judgment out of his voice. The choice was Byron's to make.

"Yeah, but I owe Darcey a lot," Byron said.

He rolled his eyes when Ronan raised an eyebrow.

"I mean it," he went on. "She's the only one in the family who's ever treated me like I was normal – not scary or embarrassing or crazy. Just *me*. And I know how the family can be around relationships, especially since she used to be 'the good one,' and if I can run interference, then I probably should."

"She can hear you, you know," Darcey sang out from a few paces behind them. "I'm still the good one!"

"Private conversation here," Byron snapped.

"In the middle of the street!"

"Shush. Adults are talking!"

"I'm twenty-three! I have a degree! You're the one with the undecided haircut and clothes that don't fit right!"

Ronan shook his head despairingly but left them to bicker.

He didn't have any cousins so he had no idea how these things worked.

He'd never really come out either, which he assumed was what Byron meant when he said the family had 'issues' with relationships.

His father had caught him reading a book on Alexander the Great one summer, and had swapped it for a far more accurate one from the locked section of his grandfather's library, with no more explanation than that 'the description of his relationship with Hephaestion is more accurate'.

That book had certainly been an education.

Grandpa Edwin himself had been far less subtle when he'd sent Ronan off to the academy with a thumbs up, and a gift box containing extra strong condoms and specialist lubricant. Sometimes Ronan wondered how he'd managed to grow up to be as mentally well-balanced as he had.

"Besides, I think I'll be able to cope with being in the grounds better if you're with me."

Ronan blinked, a rib creaking squeeze of Byron's arm breaking his reverie.

"What?" He hadn't realized he was being addressed.

"Byron doesn't like being near the spooky summer house," Darcey said, wriggling her fingers as she dragged out the vowels in 'spooky.' "Well, where the summer house *used to be* before he burnt it down like a complete fucking psycho when I was two years old and got himself sent to anger management camp."

Darcey laughed and skipped ahead of them, oblivious to the way Byron was staring stony-faced at the ground.

Something about his posture made alarm bells ring at the back of Ronan's mind.

Going to this birthday party seemed like a very bad idea.

10

THE INTERNET HAD NOT BEEN HELPFUL FOR RONAN ON THIS ONE, NOT
that he'd really expected it to be. He had no real idea what he was looking
for, just a feeling that something was very, very wrong.

He knew there were things that could offer limited protection
against a wide range of supernatural effects, but he couldn't find those
online. There were some things search engines just weren't calibrated
for, and he'd never been any good at drawing runic maps with a
computer mouse.

This was a case for tried and tested traditional methods.

Late night phone calls to dusty bookshops that looked like they'd
closed down several decades earlier. That was the ticket.

It had been years since he last did something like this, and Ronan's few
remaining contacts for supernatural matters were scattered across Europe.
Midnight on the eastern seaboard was practically bedtime for most of
them, particularly the not-quite-human ones. Since they all knew him
of old, and trusted him to always do the least harm, they gave him what
answers they could.

The majority of those answers were yet more telephone numbers, plus
a few unexpected email addresses and one 'homing pigeon address that
was almost certainly a wind up.' Still, after a dozen calls to some of the
more local numbers, he had a plan.

After the extraction of three vials of his own blood – and other more
valuable fluids – Ronan was sneaking through the moonlit streets of the
dozing city ready to complete his mission. Insofar as a person could sneak
while still using a crutch.

Despite the noise of his departure, and his return, Byron seemed to sleep through the entire thing, though Ronan's pillow was firmly jammed between his thighs when he tried to get into bed.

It was sweet that he'd missed him even in his sleep, but Ronan was grateful that he hadn't woken up.

There were some aspects of his life he wasn't ready to share just yet.

"This is your car?" Ronan asked, knowing full well he wasn't hiding the horror in his voice.

Although Byron had described 'The Fury' to him on more than one occasion, nothing he'd said had prepared Ronan for the reality.

It wasn't just that American cars were bigger than he was used to in England – Ronan had worked around tanks and troop transporters for years. The difference was those were meant to be big, and ugly. This thing was beautiful, and yet it seemed to be hunkered down in its corner of the underground garage like a very pretty but very deadly dragon. It overhung the lines of its own parking space in every direction – only motorcycles could fit in around it, and they gave off an air of fear at its proximity.

This vehicle didn't just have a personality of its own. It gave other vehicles a personality just to bully them.

"Yep," Byron said proudly. "Fury, this is Ronan. Ronan, this is my baby. I rebuilt her with my own hands."

"Are you sure you didn't accidentally get confused and build a boat?"

"Fuck off."

Ronan chuckled to himself. "Sorry, it's very impressive. You could probably have parked my last car across the nose and it wouldn't even overhang."

He stared at it some more, trying to think of something to say. He'd never been big on car culture, and he certainly didn't know anything about vehicles from the fifties. It was certainly very impressive, all swooping lines and curves, but all he really knew was that it had been in a horror film.

Finally he settled on a show of polite interest. "Aren't these cars supposed to be red?"

The Fury was black and chrome, which added to the impression that it was hiding in the shadows.

"No, they were actually only produced in cream and gold," Byron said, gesturing towards the trim on the tailfin which still had a gold inlay. "She wasn't rebuilt to the original specs. I changed the paint, the transmission, some other things. Spare parts can be hard to find."

"Airbags?"

Judging from the way Byron laughed, that was a 'no.'

"What about power steering? I mean, can you drive it right now? With your arm how it is?"

"I'll be fine," Byron nodded, "my surgeon said I was okay to drive an automatic."

"Yes, but did he say you were okay to drive an automatic *boat*?"

"Are you jealous of my car?"

Ronan wasn't going to dignify that with a direct response.

"I just don't want to end up driving that thing. Everyone's already on the wrong side of the road," he muttered. "I trained to jump out of planes, not drive a tank."

Byron patted him on the shoulder in a way that felt more condescending than reassuring.

"You won't have to drive. I'll get Darcey to do it if I need a break. It's only five hours out to the Hamptons, so I shouldn't need it."

Five hours. Ronan was going to have to get used to distances here as well. Everything was further away than it seemed.

"You should apologize to the car though."

"What?" Ronan looked at him. He couldn't tell if he was joking. "I'm not going to-"

Their corner of the parking garage suddenly filled with light.

Someone shrieked. It definitely wasn't Ronan.

The door of the car behind them opened and closed as its owner climbed inside.

"You heard them coming, didn't you?" Ronan asked once his heart rate had settled a bit. "You heard them coming and you knew their headlights would come on when they unlocked their car."

Byron just grinned.

"You absolute bastard."

"You're the one being rude to my car."

"Fine, I'm sorry I besmirched your good name, oh marvelous and benevolent Fury!" he said, complete with hand gestures and as close as he could get to a bow. "Happy now?"

"I think you were being sarcastic."

As a man more used to cramming himself into trucks with half a dozen other guys plus their own body weight in kit, the space inside the Fury felt like a luxury.

Even with four adults there was enough room to stretch out, which partially made up for the old-fashioned suspension and the rigidity of the bench-style seats. Being bounced around was nothing new, but Ronan appreciated not having someone's elbow jammed into his ribs as well.

Although he'd been told he was safe to drive, Byron hadn't been out in the Fury since he got out of the hospital – apparently, he didn't like using it in the city and preferred to run wherever he could. Ronan certainly wouldn't be doing the same, assuming his knees ever recovered that far.

It wasn't that he didn't want to be fit, but rather that taxis existed for a reason. In this case that reason was 'to let someone else deal with the traffic.'

For someone who loved his car, Byron did not like other drivers.

Ronan had worried that having two relative strangers along on their first road trip might make the situation a little tense, but the women proved to be a very welcome distraction from Byron's road rage.

To say it was bad would be an understatement. Almost the instant they pulled out of the parking garage Byron was slinging insults so varied that he was using swear words Ronan had never even heard before.

Although Byron never progressed to threatening anything physical against the other occupants of the road, it was still a relief to be able to turn around and talk to someone with a better grip on their sanity.

Darcey's girlfriend Astrid had grown up as a military child just like him, though she'd travelled with her parents through various Canadian Air Force bases rather than being sent to a residential school. They'd spent an enjoyable half hour debating the pros and cons of military versus commercial flight – Astrid had never considered the military for herself, preferring to fly small commercial transports, while Ronan had rejected parachuting just for leisure. Not that Ronan could do either any more.

Meanwhile Darcey had been raised on her mother's farm somewhere in the middle of Ohio, which was next to her father Marco's small commercial airstrip.

The official story about the beginning of Marco's business was that – rather than intentionally joining the aviation industry – Marco had won the whole place in a card game during a visit to Atlantic City.

Quite sensibly, his sister Gianna hadn't believed a word of it until he took her out to Ohio to see the place in the flesh. Whether she ever believed the origin story wasn't clear since she was immediately distracted by another matter. Around 3am of her first night staying at Marco's new home, a young and attractive David Williams had accidentally walked into her bedroom half-asleep and half-naked after a late-night run from Paraguay.

"The rest, as they say, is history," Darcey said with a laugh when Byron cringed at the tale of his parent's first meeting. "Of course, no one talks about what David may or may not have been transporting at that point."

"Gamblers, smugglers, and thieves," he said darkly.

"Hey, that's one third not true," Darcey cut in. "Unless you've been stealing."

Astrid threw a balled-up candy wrapper at her girlfriend. "We run a legitimate business!"

Byron shook his head. "Yeah, *now you do*. That's all Star's influence. I'm sure Gianna wanted them to go straight, but it was Star who put his foot down."

"Star?" Ronan was sure he'd heard that name before, but he couldn't place it.

"My other dad," Darcey added. "My mom wanted a kid without the hassle of getting married, my dad wanted a family but he's not into girls. Star was his call sign in the air force, it's a pun because his surname is Reising."

"Just like my boyfriend – Roaming Cocks."

"Fuck off," Ronan snapped back, more out of habit than actual annoyance. He'd almost asked if this was the guy Byron had once mentioned pushing down the stairs, but if he was Darcey's dad that would probably be a sore topic.

"So, everyone in your family met through your dad's workplace, then?" he asked Darcey instead. "You and Astrid, Gianna and David, your parents, Star and your dad?"

Darcey nodded.

"Why are you worried about your family's reaction then?"

"I'm supposed to be the good one who goes back to college, gets a Masters, and a fancy job," she said. Although she was talking to Ronan her eyes were fixed on the back of Byron's head as she spoke. "I'm in the scientific field, but everyone's hoping I'll eventually go into business via R&D or something. From there it wouldn't be too much of a leap to take over Gianna's business. If I decide to go back to Ohio and do aviation repairs for the rest of my life then the business will just have to be sold."

Everyone in the car jumped when Byron laid heavily on the horn and swerved around a minivan. It might have been a coincidence, but judging by the way his knuckles stayed white on the steering wheel, Byron was directing his anger outward.

Ronan had no idea how to address the subject of Byron being disinherited from his own mother's company while she still seemed to be in good health. Did the entire family really believe he'd never be capable of the responsibility? So much so that they were making the decision now? What had Byron done to deserve that? Didn't most parents believe that their children could grow and improve?

No, Ronan had met Gianna – she seemed to think Byron was still a child.

They'd have to talk about that in private.

To Darcey he said, "It's always good to have a career plan, but don't set things in stone when you're young. I expected to retire from the military into a teaching job and keep doing jumps into my fifties. Now I'm not even allowed to kneel, let alone jump out of a plane. Plus, you've not been dating for long, right?"

"Oh, not long. Only for two years," Astrid said in a tone that suggested this was very much a point of contention between the two of them.

"Yeah, Marco is going to kill you," Byron muttered.

"Which is why I need you there to make a distraction."

"Well that's all I'm good for, apparently."

"Anyway," Astrid said loudly over what was sure to turn into a fight, "Ronan, what do you think of America so far?"

Grateful for the subject change, Ronan launched into the comparison of anything he could think of, reaching out to put a hand on Byron's knee as he spoke. Byron was so tense he was shaking.

Ronan had no idea if it would help, but he tried to think appreciative thoughts as loudly as he could for the rest of the journey.

Byron wasn't just a distraction for him.

Although he'd spent plenty of summers in a literal manor house – one that was so old that parts of the foundations predated the Domesday Book – Ronan had not been expecting the scale of Byron's family home.

Yes, his grandfather's house had technically contained seven bedrooms, but only three of them were livable, and parts of the roof had been missing for longer than Ronan had been alive. By comparison the Williams residence looked like a palace.

It was hard to believe that it wasn't a movie set, but he'd thought the same thing about almost every house they'd passed during the last half-hour.

There were no other members of the Williams family at the house when they arrived, just a team of harassed staff running around trying to set up for the party to Gianna's exacting standards.

The event itself would be taking place the next day, but Gianna wanted the family to have brunch together in the morning as a more intimate celebration before the three hundred guests arrived for the evening party. As such, Marco, Gianna, and David would be arriving by nightfall, but until then the younger people would have 'free' rein of the house.

It seemed that Gianna's definition of 'free' wasn't the same as anyone else's.

Instructions had been left to put Byron in his childhood room with Darcey next door and their 'guests' in another wing entirely.

There were a lot of air quotes involved in the directions from Gianna's personal assistant. Ronan couldn't tell if it was supposed to be sarcasm or if she'd actually been told to talk like that. Either way there was no point getting involved in an argument with an employee over the legitimacy of his relationship.

He just ignored her instead, and walked straight back to Byron's room the moment the woman went back downstairs. He couldn't help but laugh when Astrid did the same.

However, his laughter died in his throat when Byron opened his bedroom door.

Ronan hadn't seen inside on the initial tour – the assistant had practically run them out of that part of the house.

The best word he could use to describe Byron's room was 'disturbing.' It was white. Entirely white. Everything – walls, floors, furniture, soft furnishings – every single surface was stark, brilliant white. It was clear this wasn't an artistic choice.

What he'd seen of the house so far, even the guest rooms, had been styled with objects that oozed opulence despite their simplicity. The decor in Byron's room – white chipboard furniture, motel-quality sheets, linoleum floor – looked like it had been purchased with easy replacement in mind.

Walking into that room felt like stepping into a different building.

Ronan closed the door, counted to five, and opened it again. It still opened into the same corridor. Probably not a portal then, which, in a way, was much worse.

Why would anyone so completely erase their son's existence from their lives, and then make him look at that erasure? Why not just redecorate it like the rest of the house?

"I guess throwing out all your stuff isn't any weirder than Grandpa Edwin leaving my bedroom exactly how it was for five years after I joined the army," he said in a poor attempt to cover his discomfort. "Why'd they paint it white though?"

"This is how I left it," Byron said quietly, poking the toe of his boot at a rug that was barely more than white hessian.

That seemed hard to believe.

Ronan couldn't imagine Byron – with his bright green highlights and colorful tattoos – growing up in this nightmarishly blank space.

Now he understood part of what Byron had told him about running away from home. He'd mentioned never being allowed to interact with things that were too 'stimulating,' but Ronan had assumed that was hyperbole. His own father hadn't let him watch shows he considered 'vulgar,' so he'd thought that Byron's parents had done much the same. He'd hadn't expected this sort of sensory deprivation.

"They really made you live in here? All your life?"

"Not all my life." Byron still wasn't looking at him. His head was shifting oddly from side to side as he walked around the room, almost like a swimmer trying to dislodge water from his ears. "It started slow. After the fire they took away all my comic books. Then my action figures. They thought they were a bad influence. When the first behavioral camp didn't work out, they started changing more things. Gianna said I was overstimulated, even though my teachers said I was acting out. I drew things that scared her, so she took my pens. I used words she didn't like, so she took my books. I'd get better when I was away, get worse when I came back. I don't even remember what I did to lose colored clothes. She replaced everything with plain blue jeans and grey shirts but it didn't matter because I was rarely at home by then. Everywhere they sent me had a uniform."

"Bloody hell." There wasn't really anything else Ronan could say to it all. It sounded like abuse, but he still didn't know what exactly Byron had done to trigger all of this.

It was hard to imagine Byron actually doing anything bad, certainly not now that he knew him. He was tall, wide, and muscular but that didn't mean anything – 'gentle giant' was a trope for a reason. Ronan had rarely seen him angry, and he couldn't think of any time he'd used violence without provocation. When they were together, he used his strength to hold Ronan up, not bring anyone down.

He could see why people might take the tattoos and gothic fashion as something of a threat, but standing in this bare room all of that seemed inevitable. It was only natural that anyone raised in this room would have rebelled – it was that or go mad. But by all accounts, 'the fire' had been first.

"Knock, knock," Darcey said from the doorway. Ronan's questions would have to wait until later. "Whoa, this place is as horrible as I remembered, wanna go raid the wine cellar?"

"No, but I'll break into David's liquor cabinet for you," Byron said.

He was smiling, but it was clear to Ronan that the expression was a mask.

The rest of the house was just as oddly pristine as it had looked from the outside. It was like a show home, or a movie set that was trying to convey that people with money owned the property but didn't really live there.

There were no signs of wear on the furniture. Every surface was covered in beautiful knickknacks, but no personal effects. Even the art on the walls looked like it had been chosen for either value, or color coordination.

A few professional photographs of the family were displayed on the shelves, but there wasn't a single candid shot amongst them. The only picture of Byron that Ronan saw anywhere in the house was a huge studio portrait of a toddler in a sailor suit with caramel-brown hair. Ronan only recognized it by a distinctive collection of moles on his neck.

There were also no images of anyone from the generation before Gianna and Marco, which was a strange omission for a family as well-off as this one. A number of Ronan's ancestors had been traitors to the crown, but his grandfather would never have hidden their portraits away.

Byron seemed as bothered by the decor as Ronan – he moved something in every room they passed through, tipping over vases and pulling books off shelves. He didn't always use his hands, and Ronan wondered how Darcey and Astrid never noticed things like the curtains untying themselves.

In David's office – or at least Ronan assumed that's who the impersonal room belonged to – Byron unlocked the liquor cabinet with a touch and handed out bottles of twenty-year-old scotch like it was soda.

Ronan put the one he was offered back.

He didn't want to get drunk right now.

When the women left the room in the direction of the terrace, Byron quietly returned his own bottle, too. Ronan took his hand, but didn't say anything.

It didn't feel like words would help.

They abandoned their tour of the house after the third time one of them hit their head on the light fittings above the kitchen counters. It seemed that his parents had remodeled that part of the house since Byron left, and Gianna had designed things to suit her own short stature rather than the taller male members of the family.

Ronan insisted they go outside before somebody lost an eye.

The gardens had a manicured feel that spoke of a hidden army of gardeners who probably appeared in the early morning to trim an extra millimeter off the grass every day. Ronan's grandfather had a flock of sheep to do the job instead. He couldn't imagine Gianna dealing with livestock occasionally wandering onto the veranda.

Beyond the lawn – which was dotted with marquees and half-decorated buffet tables – there was a pool, then a tennis court, then finally an oddly dense area of woodland.

Most of the houses in the area seemed to have a privacy screen of trees around the edges of their property, but something about this patch of forest felt different. The front section of trees was clearly much younger than the back. Ronan had reluctantly learned some land management skills on his grandfather's estate. He recognized artificial planting patterns when he saw them.

Byron stopped by the pool and turned back to look at the house. Ronan followed his gaze, but he couldn't see what he was looking at – the staff were still bustling everywhere, Darcey and Astrid were sitting under an umbrella bigger than Byron's bedroom, nothing seemed out of place.

"What's with the trees?" Ronan asked.

If Byron heard him, he gave no sign of it.

When it became clear that Byron wasn't going to acknowledge him, or move from his current spot, Ronan continued on his own.

Pinecones and twigs made the ground hard going with a single crutch, rather than the two he'd been using in D.C. He knew he was supposed to be reducing the amount of support he used, but his doctors probably hadn't meant for him to go hiking any time soon.

Using the word hiking to describe walking in a private garden should have been an exaggeration, but as soon as Ronan was under the shadow of the trees, he felt like he was somewhere else. It was almost the same feeling as being in Byron's room. Intellectually he knew that if he looked back the house would still be in view, but as long as he kept moving forward that didn't feel true.

The layer of recent trees only extended back about thirty feet. After that the plants started to thin out again quite abruptly, with yellowing plastic grow tubes appearing among the undergrowth where new trees had been planted but had failed to thrive. Soon there was no undergrowth at all, only tubes and scruffy clumps of grass that seemed to be barely holding onto life.

At the center of this abnormal clearing, like a meteorite at the bottom of its extinction-triggering crater, was a twenty-foot square patch of ruined earth. Fire-blackened and utterly dead, its clear outline was unexpected given the density and age of the trees around it – after a decade or two of New England winters there should have been some reclamation of the soil. Even if nothing could grow there, Ronan would have expected a layer of leaf mould to soften the edges and provide some life support for mushrooms or lichen.

Standing even at arm's length from that space seemed like a very bad choice.

The wind shifted.

Someone nearby was having a bonfire.

Ronan could smell burning bones.

He didn't run. He *couldn't* run, but even if he could have done, he wasn't that stupid. He turned as best he could and walked, at a sensible, dignified pace, away from whatever the hell was in that clearing.

Byron was waiting where he'd left him.

He took Ronan's hand when it was offered, but something wasn't right about him.

Ronan kept his hand clamped over the objects in his pocket all the way back to the house.

11

Dinner was a stilted, awkward affair.

David and Marco, with Star in tow, had arrived just before nightfall, while Gianna had got tangled up in some urgent work, and had insisted they eat without her while she drove back from New York.

Byron's father was not the man Ronan had been expecting. The portrait Byron had painted was of a neglectful, aloof disciplinarian – one of those hard-edged men who'd made the move from small-time criminal to wearing Armani suits that barely covered their prison tattoos. That image couldn't have been further from the truth.

Instead he looked like a tall handsome cowboy who'd wandered into a Hawaiian shirt store, but had still managed to find something the color of denim. He was affable and funny with a story to tell for every comment. The only hint that he wasn't entirely happy was the way he stared at Byron whenever the conversation moved away from his input.

Beside him Mac laughed dutifully at every joke, a true sidekick to David's larger personality. He seemed well, and eager to eat as much of the food as he could reach. Ronan tried once or twice to make polite conversation with him. Usually he was better at faking these things, but it was hard when his brain kept pointing out that this man was a shapeshifter. Byron was no help – he barely spoke to anyone at all.

Meanwhile, Astrid seemed to be a little drunk, and soon frightened herself into silence after giggling at one of Marco's comments that hadn't actually been a joke. It couldn't have been fun being trapped across the table from your girlfriend's father who is also your boss.

Even though he was a guest himself, Ronan tried his best to engage the whole table with aviation topics, since he knew they all shared history in that field. Most answers turned into David sharing yet another anecdote, and the rest of the table nodding dutifully along while Byron sank further into his chair.

By 9 pm Ronan played the disability card for possibly the first time since his injuries, and insisted they go to bed.

It said something about the quality of the evening that closing the door into that weird white room was a relief.

At least Byron's parents had let him have a double bed.

There was no way the two of them would have been able to fit in a single bed, but damn it, Ronan would have tried anyway.

He was so tired he was almost asleep on his feet.

"What's that?" Byron muttered as Ronan emptied his pockets onto the nightstand.

Keys, phone, wallet, pain medication, 'sugar packets' that had taken three hours to track down, and finally – the object.

Byron poked it. "Looks almost like the head off a flail."

"Do you relate everything to weapons?" Ronan deflected.

He didn't really want to talk to Byron about the palm sized clump of metal pieces right now. He should have kept it in his pocket until he was finished changing for bed.

"Ha!" That wasn't a laugh, it was the empty sound of someone who was too depressed to be amused and knew people would worry if he didn't fake it.

"I suppose you could use it as a flail," Ronan said with feigned disinterest. "It's just a good luck charm my grandfather gave me."

That was a lie. One he was sure Byron would have picked up on if Ronan hadn't chosen that precise moment to wrap his arms around Byron's shoulders and pull him in for a kiss.

Falling into Byron's childhood bed together felt risqué, like they were fumbling teens rather than grown men in full control of their lives. They were both too tired – and too stressed – to do much, but in the dark, they still managed to find the relief that would finally let them sleep.

He didn't like sleepovers.

Ronan had never had a sleepover in his life. He'd shared plenty of dormitories but he'd never invited any children to his grandfather's house, nor had he ever been invited to one.

He didn't want to have a stupid sleepover with all these stupid people in the first place.

Ah, so this was a dream.

They weren't his friends anyway; they were just the children of his mom's stuck-up friends.

He'd never called his mother 'mom.' Was this *his* dream?

Even as Ronan asked himself that question, the discontented monologue rolled on.

He couldn't even remember all their names and now he had to lay on the hard, wooden floor of this stupid, drafty, spider-infested summer house, listening to them snoring while he didn't get any sleep at all.

Somewhere far away the hairs on Ronan's neck stood on end at 'summer house.'

It wasn't fair.

"Kill them, then."

What? Where had that thought come from? Was it a thought, or was it a voice?

Ronan tried to say that the words hadn't come from him, but he couldn't make a sound.

The words had seemed so...calm. Reasonable. Caring.

What? No! Where the hell was he? Why the fuck would he think a murderous disembodied voice was being reasonable?

"Oh, they don't like you any more than you like them, poppet. They're all scared of you. They've heard about your special little talents. They all think you're a witch. Your mother paid their parents to bring them here. You deserve better than that, don't you?"

No, they're here because mom has a very important job and their parents have to meet to talk about business. Tomorrow there's going to be a party. With cake.

"Really now poppet, that was just a lie your mother told you so you would sleep out here."

He wanted to say no again, but mommy did lie a lot. She always said they'd have fun together tomorrow, but tomorrow never came.

Ronan tried to scream, tried to move, tried to do anything to make Byron wake up.

"My darling child, you know they'll never play with you. Not really. They can't understand you, poppet, not the way I can. They talk about you when you're not around. They don't trust you. I'm afraid they want to hurt you."

He looked around the room at the sleeping boys, his gaze skipping over the bigger form of Aurelio, five years his senior and so, so handsome with his big dark eyes. Everyone liked Aurelio. No one liked Ben.

I like you, Ronan thought as loud as he could. He knew it made no difference.

He stared at the others, the strangers. Should he, *could* he, kill them? Why? Why did he want to do that?

"Don't you want someone to love you?" Breath ghosted across his ears – one side hot, the other impossibly cold – as if two people were leaning against his shoulders. "Don't you want someone who can understand you?"

Icy hands with the texture of twigs were touching him. Touching his hair, touching his face, his chest, his back, pressing into his mouth, pulling at his clothes, touching places no one was ever supposed to touch.

Where before Ronan had felt only his own fear and Byron's reflected terror, now his mind turned to rage. How dare? He could feel his teeth grinding somewhere else, somewhere that wasn't here.

Enough.

"Kill them and I can be real, poppet, I can love you like you deserve. I can show you everything you could ever want to know about who you are."

He wanted to scream but there was a weight crushing his chest, iron bands closing around his throat, so hot they burned, and he didn't know whether these were Byron's thoughts or his own any more.

He couldn't breathe.

"Come on, poppet, kill them for me. You deserve so much more. Kill *him* for me, make me real, set me free–"

There was paper on his tongue.

Skeletal hands creeping down his thighs. No. The hands were flesh-

and-blood, and they were crushing his windpipe, or were they thin and prising at his teeth?

He didn't know.

Who was he?

His name was Byron, not Ben, not Poppet. Byron.

The paper dissolved, spilling salt and silver across his tongue, where it burned and burned and burned.

He opened his mouth to spit. A ball of jagged metal was forced between his teeth.

He tried to scream but the mass just sliced into his flesh, where it burned like a magnesium fire, too much, too much to take inside this frail human body.

Something left, as fast and as violently as it had arrived, leaving ashes in its wake.

In that horrible white bedroom Byron collapsed unconscious across Ronan's struggling form.

Gasping for breath took all his strength, but Ronan managed to shove the huge man up and off him with one great heave of his trembling, oxygen-starved arms.

He landed squarely on the thin hessian rug, and Ronan thanked whatever gods had been watching for that one small mercy.

Ronan could see his own reflection in the bathroom mirror from where he sat on the edge of the cheap motel bed.

He wished he couldn't.

He looked like shit.

How he'd managed to convince the front desk clerk to rent him a room in this state he might never know. The fact that he'd also successfully hauled Byron from the back of the Fury into the room without arousing suspicion was probably proof of the existence of some kind of deity. Or that this was a very bad motel.

If Ronan looked like shit, then Byron looked no better. There was dried blood all over his face and chest where it had drooled out of his mouth from the cuts Ronan's protective spell had left behind.

Four or more of Byron's teeth had been chipped or broken in the process of getting the damn amulet assemblage between his jaws. Ronan had been badly bitten in the process, but he knew if he hadn't managed to toss the 'sugar packet' in there first he'd probably have lost a finger.

The old tricks really were the best.

Absently he stroked Byron's hair where the man slept fitfully behind him, his other hand coming up to rest against his own throat.

The deep red marks from Byron's fingers were starting to darken to purple now, and Ronan wasn't sure how he was going to hide them from the others at the party tomorrow. They'd have to go back to the house early, before anyone came to their room to wake them. It would be a disaster if anyone found them missing, with nothing but blood and semen-stained sheets left behind. Better that Byron show up with a ruined mouth and a battered boyfriend, than accidentally look like a murderer.

Or a murder victim.

He looked terrible. He hadn't woken yet and Ronan still needed to assess the extent of his injuries. Hell, he still needed to get the spell back out of his mouth.

Whatever had possessed him hadn't followed them beyond the bounds of the property. Ronan had felt it withdrawing while he bundled his half-naked boyfriend into the back of the unfamiliar car, in a country he'd never driven in before.

Perhaps the thing had just not wanted to risk his driving.

More likely it couldn't leave. Hadn't Byron talked about getting better every time he was sent away from home as a child? That seemed to prove that the thing was limited to one location.

If they went back Ronan would have to keep a careful eye on Byron the entire time they were on the property.

There was no way in hell Ronan would ever let them sleep there again. Even after he arranged for someone more experienced to exorcise the damn place. He wasn't even sure that would work.

Again, his mind went back to Byron's wounds. He needed to see which of the amulets had burnt the most so he could work out who to actually contact to remove the spirit, demon, monster, arsehole-who'd-dared-to-possess-his-boyfriend.

He'd spent his whole life dealing with creatures whose opinions on humanity ranged from fond curiosity to burning hatred.

He had absolutely no sympathy for a thing that would possess and molest a child, try to compel him to murder other children, and then torment that child for decades. That was pure evil.

He'd do anything he could so they'd be free to live their life together in peace.

Someone needed to be on Byron's side in this world.

'Why does my mouth taste like blood and fear?'

The thought wasn't his own. Despite last night's melodrama, Ronan still felt a wave of relief at hearing Byron's voice in his head. He sounded *right* this time, like his usual adult self rather than a frightened child.

'What did I do this time?'

The question was followed by a dizzying montage of images. Bloody knuckles, broken windows, burning cars, ruined meals, empty psychiatric wards. The only thing Ronan recognized among the horror was the figure of Star Reising tumbling down a long flight of stairs.

For a moment he had to grab the edge of the sink to keep himself upright as Byron's various pains overlaid his own. Combined with the aching of his knees after last night's abuse it was almost enough to knock him to the floor.

Of course, Ronan already knew Byron's mouth was a mess – he felt terrible about doing that – but it seemed he'd done a poor job of moving him to the car, too. Byron's arm ached and he was intensely aware of the tightness in his face.

Whether Byron had felt Ronan's pain as well, or if his brain had finally woken up enough to catch up with current events, he suddenly seemed to notice his absence.

'Ronan?'

In the next room the bed creaked. The sound was followed by a groan. Perhaps he was trying to sit up. Ronan wasn't sure he wanted to be seen just yet.

'Ronan?' This time his name was accompanied by a blind sort of panic and the image of how they'd fallen asleep with Ronan tucked close against Byron's side.

What the hell was he thinking, to leave him to that fear?

Ronan pushed open the bathroom door and almost instantly regretted it. He'd left the other room in darkness so Byron could rest, which meant he was now backlit like some kind of serial killer.

"Hey," he tried to say, but it came out more like a death rattle.

Sitting up on top of the rumpled bed sheets, still covered in dried blood almost to the waist, Byron was staring at him with a look of horror.

In an effort to be reassuring, Ronan stepped forward with a hand outstretched, the universal signal for calm he'd used so many times before. He knew it was a mistake as soon he got within a few feet of Byron and a memory of grasping skeletal hands overlaid his vision.

He wasn't fast enough to step back.

Byron's grip was so tight Ronan would swear the bones of his wrist were grinding together as his arm was twisted away from him.

In direct contradiction to instincts and training, he forced his forearm to relax.

He coughed, but managed to grate out the words, "Byron? Could you let me go, please?"

"Woahnan? Wah..." was far as Byron made it through a reply.

"Now please, while I can still feel my fingers."

Byron let go.

'Have I been chewing glass?' he asked, returning to thoughts instead of spoken words.

As a deliberate, rather than accidental, projection Byron's mental voice now had a completely different tone. He sounded harder somehow, and Ronan wasn't sure if he preferred it.

Sitting carefully on the edge of the mattress, Ronan waited until Byron seemed to be relaxed before reaching out toward his face again. Byron shrank back. He stopped.

Ronan knew that being a silhouette wasn't helping the situation, but turning the lights on by the bed would be even worse. He'd rather Byron not be able to see his face than have him see what he'd done to Ronan's neck.

"I need to look at your mouth," Ronan said, trying not to cringe at the rusty gate crackle that still blurred every word. "It's important, Byron, please."

'Stop using my name like that. Like you're trying to calm a wounded animal.'

"Aren't I?"

Byron was almost screaming now inside their heads. The behavior didn't exactly encourage being treated like a rational adult. Especially when he shifted further and further up the bed every time Ronan spoke.

'Why do you sound like that?' Byron asked, though if by coincidence or telepathy Ronan couldn't tell. 'Why are the lights off? If I can't see you, how do I know you're *you*?'

"Can't you just, I don't know, doesn't the inside of my head feel different?"

'I'm not in your head.'

The instant denial was too much. Ronan reached forward and gripped his boyfriend's knee where it was curled defensively in front of him.

"Byron, I felt you waking up."

'Oh.'

The movement was hesitant at first, but slowly Byron covered Ronan's hand with his own.

When nothing bad happened after the first seconds he gently ran his hand up along the outstretched arm to a slim shoulder, and from there to a bearded cheek.

Ronan smiled to himself as Byron thought the word 'warm' with a palpable feeling of relief.

He sat patiently while he mapped the contours of sharp cheekbones and a rounded jaw line. He let him trace the laughter lines half hidden by his beard.

When his fingers reached his lips, Ronan pressed a kiss to Byron's thumb. "Better?"

"Mm hmm," Byron mumbled.

"Okay, well, you need to let me look at your mouth now," Ronan said, and leaned forward to grip Byron's jaw. It was hard to break such a sweet moment, but he had to be practical.

Perhaps surprised into obedience, Byron opened his mouth, blinking hard as the torch on Ronan's phone shone in his eyes for a moment before it was redirected to its proper target.

Ronan made a few thoughtful noises, turning Byron's head this way and that as he angled the light.

"Well, there's a lot of cuts and you've five chipped teeth, but I don't think anything needs stitches and the teeth might be able to wait." He pressed two cups into Byron's hands, one warm and full, the other empty. "Here, swill this around your mouth then spit it out into the other cup. It might take you a few rounds to get through the whole cup. Then I'll check again but I think you'll be fine."

Byron took a sip, then half choked at the taste.

'What the hell is this? This is salt! Urgh, that much salt cannot be healthy!'

"That's why I said swill with it!" Ronan exclaimed, his voice cracking horribly on the aspirated consonant.

He paused to cough again before continuing more carefully. "Salt water is the best way to clean mouth wounds but you're not supposed to drink it."

"'kay."

They sat in silence, Ronan fitfully rubbing his hand over Byron's knee while he swished the warm saline around his mouth and flinched at every sting. It seemed that concentrating on the task calmed Byron enough for his legs to gradually relax. It wasn't enough for Ronan to hold him yet, but it was a start.

"How do you feel?" Ronan asked once the cup was empty.

When he took it from Byron's hand, he instinctively pressed the back of his free hand briefly against Byron's forehead in a gesture that felt like a mother hen, but oddly tender at the same time.

Much to his relief Byron leaned in.

He tried to speak out loud but soon gave up in favor of thinking again – he couldn't enunciate much in this state.

'Like I ate broken glass. Please, why won't you tell me what I did?'

"It's okay Byron, no one was hurt," Ronan said slowly. He knew he sounded like he was trying to fake cheerfulness but his distorted voice spoiled the effect.

'Stop doing that with my name.'

Ronan ploughed on, regardless. "Thankfully, no one saw me dragging you out of there on a rug in nothing but your underpants. I just have to hope that no one checks your room before we get back because there's quite a lot of blood on those sheets."

Byron's thoughts were almost a scream. 'WHAT DID I DO?'

"Nothing. *You* didn't do anything, but when it became clear that the thing in your body wasn't you – I had to get rid of it. It's a good thing I always come prepared."

"Wha?" Apparently, Byron was so confused by that statement he forgot that it hurt to speak.

Scrabbling around in the dark amongst the mess on the bedside table Ronan eventually found the sticky, jagged mass of metal he was looking for. "Do you remember asking about my keychain?"

Byron nodded. "Yeath."

"It's exactly what it looks like," he said, poking at the various charms to separate them.

'Well, it looks like a robotic hedgehog,' Byron thought darkly, the attempt at humor completely failing to cover his mistrust.

"This is nearly a hundred blessed, sacred, and sanctified symbols from as many belief systems as I could possibly find, all strung together into a ball with silver wire." Ronan hefted his creation and smiled grimly at the weight. "If an exorcism is a precision strike against a single demon, this is an occult hand grenade addressed 'to whom it may concern.' It would also work against most normal humans as well, if you swing it hard enough."

'And you put that in *my mouth*?'

Perhaps he wasn't being quite as reassuring as he could be.

"The mouth is a great way to get a large surface area of flesh into contact with as many symbols as possible. Plus, your mouth is pretty sensitive, and once this gets past your teeth..." Ronan trailed off there. He still felt somewhat bad about how much force he'd had to use.

Byron swallowed, then grimaced at the pain.

"It's so big you can't spit it out," Ronan finished. "I mean, ideally a person would hold it in their hand but your hands were busy, so that was the best available option. I couldn't see clearly when I pulled it out, but I think a few of the symbols burned as well as cut you. I'll take some photos when it's light enough and that might give us a clue about the nature of the thing that got into your head."

"'Speth."

The word was said so quietly that Ronan initially thought he'd heard someone speaking in the next room. If Byron hadn't started to curl in on himself Ronan might never have realized where the sound came from.

"What?"

'That thing. In my head. She...it told me its name was Else Peth.'

"Elspeth?" Ronan asked. Byron had pronounced the name as two words rather than one.

'Could be.'

It was a Scottish name that rang a very small bell in Ronan's memory. Something to do with the witch trials perhaps? Was this the right area for that sort of thing? He needed to do some research.

"Have you ever spoken to it?" he prompted. "Can you tell me what happened? Originally, I mean?"

The silence was telling.

"You don't have to say anything if you don't want to," Ronan began, but Byron took a deep breath.

'Could you come sit up here? Next to me? Please, I don't like...'

"Sure."

Half for reassurance, and half for physical support Ronan kept his hand on Byron's knee as he carefully switched positions to sit against the headboard.

Before he was properly settled, Byron shifted to rest his head on Ronan's thigh and wrapped his arms around his waist.

At this angle he still couldn't see Ronan's face, but in the light from the bathroom Ronan could just about see Byron's expressions. If he seemed to get too distressed, he could run a hand over his bicep, or through his hair. Anything to remind him that he was still there.

Byron presented his answer as memories rather than words.

It was disorientating but Ronan could understand his reasoning – images were easier to share than to describe and there would be less room for misinterpretation. Ronan would see what Byron had seen.

Unfortunately, these images were delivered in a rush and prioritized by a traumatized mind.

Blue and red flashing lights reflecting on pool water; a moon half hidden by clouds and rising smoke; barren doctor's offices that smelled of disinfectant; serious men speaking while he stared at shoes that didn't yet reach the floor. His mother laughing and shaking her head at the idea of imaginary friends; Gianna pacing the same room but with fresh grey streaks in her dark brown hair, lecturing him about delusions. His father shouting at him to snap out of it. His uncle telling him to stop daydreaming. A toddler Ronan recognized as Darcey sobbing and sliding unnaturally across the ground as a sheet of metal fell a few inches from her head.

More empty offices; more serious voices; bars across windows; wire mesh around the perimeters of playgrounds that looked like prison yards; trays of pills and gentle voices lying that everything would be all right.

Across it all, the taste of blood and the scent of burning pine.

"I understand this must be hard for you, what you've shown me is horrible, but can you start at the beginning?" Ronan asked quietly as the parade of cell-like rooms continued.

The first image was the backyard of a different, smaller house, one with a tire swing hanging in an old oak tree and a laughing man dressed as a cowboy who threw a ball to him. Behind him a woman who barely looked like Gianna held a baby on her knee while another man talked animatedly to them both. It was hard to tell with his back turned but it was probably Marco.

He shouldn't have been able to catch the ball. It sailed past two feet away from him. His father always threw wider than his short stature could possibly reach.

That wasn't fair, he thought, and so the ball abruptly curved through the air to land in his hand.

His father didn't notice the trick.

"Ben, you're gonna be a star!" he said instead.

The pride the boy felt seemed alien now.

His schoolmates were not as forgiving. They paid attention and they knew he was cheating at whatever game they played. They didn't like it, but he disliked losing more than he disliked the looks they gave him.

The family moved.

Gianna's company was taking off, and to Ben it was as if she had all the money in the world.

They decided to host a week-long housewarming party.

Ben didn't like the new house. He didn't like the voice that spoke to him every time he went into the garden, and he didn't like the way his mother laughed at him for talking about it.

Still, he was looking forward to the party, to a chance to impress new people, and raid all the buffet tables.

He hadn't expected the children he knew at his last school to show up with their parents. He knew they were whispering to his new neighbors and telling tales about him.

He tried to hide from them, only to be told that all the children were being sent to the summer house for the night. It was supposed to be a sleepover. It was supposed to be fun.

Ronan had seen this part, though he hadn't been able to concentrate on it while he was fighting to stay alive.

Judging from the images, Byron didn't remember it all either. The memory had a hazy strobing effect to it, as if he'd been fading in and out of consciousness. He remembered a voice telling him to kill the other children. He remembered inhuman hands touching him and trying to control him at the same time. It was perverse.

Byron seemed to think he'd lost control, but Ronan could feel him resisting. Even as a child Byron hadn't actually been taken over completely – he'd picked up a baseball bat as a weapon as slowly as if he'd been moving through molasses. He'd made enough noise walking to where Aurelio was sleeping to wake the boy up. He hadn't resisted when Aurelio hit him with a chair.

The other children had woken up then, terrified by Aurelio's screaming, and the blood pouring from Ben's face. Whether anyone else heard the voice laughing wasn't clear.

Something caught fire.

Afterwards the children accused Ben of trying to burn them alive while they slept. Their narrative was that he started the fire and *then* attacked

Aurelio. The memory wasn't clear but Byron didn't seem to be near the fire when it started. It started on its own. Or perhaps it started from a thought.

Pyrokinesis was only a step from telekinesis if one thought in terms of friction, as Byron had learned when he was older. He *could* start a fire, but he'd never done it unintentionally. He didn't believe he had started the fire in the summer house either.

What he believed didn't matter.

Ben hadn't stood up for himself.

In the chaos that followed he never denied what they said had happened. He'd only stood there – covered in blood, weapon in hand – while the building burned. As the tallest, Aurelio had been able to smash a window and start ferrying the other children outside so that by the time the adults arrived Ben was the only one left. He probably wouldn't have saved himself if David hadn't dragged him out.

When the fire marshal accused him of arson he just shrugged.

Two days later he attacked one of Gianna's friends with a kitchen knife.

That was the first time he was sent away for his mental health.

That was the beginning of a decade-long downward spiral that only ended when he ran away.

Ronan tried to give Byron a comforting squeeze when he started to shake with frustration, but something about the pressure change made him look around for the first time in nearly an hour.

'What happened to your hands?' Byron asked, an edge of panic returning to his thoughts.

His eyes must have adjusted to the dark.

"Nothing."

'That's not nothing. Those are bite marks. I bit you, didn't I? I broke the skin. Why is it *yellow*?'

"Don't worry, it's just iodine," Ronan replied, as casually as he could. He almost used Byron's name again but that wouldn't have the soothing effect he wanted. "I've always got a first aid kit with me somewhere."

'That doesn't make this okay.'

Byron shook his head, then sighed so heavily that Ronan felt the bed shift with the force of it.

'Why are we still sitting in the dark?'

He'd wriggled out of Ronan's arms, and hit the light switch by the bed before Ronan could properly react. They ended up frozen face-to-face, each with a hand outstretched.

Ronan had already seen the extent of Byron's injuries, but seeing them again with the maturing bruises standing out so dark under the harsh motel light was still a shock. It would look worse before it got better. There was no way they could let Byron's parents see him like that.

As for his own injuries, he'd had plenty of time to study them in the bathroom mirror. He hadn't had a plan for revealing them to Byron. Part of him had naively hoped they could just sit in the dark until the whole thing blew over. It was a stupid fantasy to have, but there was no kind way to tell someone the handprints around your neck were their own.

'Your eyes.'

Ronan let his eyelashes flutter down of their own accord. He'd almost forgotten the hemorrhaging that had stained the whites of his eyes half red.

"You didn't do this," he said. He still couldn't speak clearly. It felt like an accusation all its own.

Byron whined deep his throat, backing away down the bed.

'You said my hands were "busy," not that I was trying to kill you.'

"You didn't do this, it was that thing, it was Elspeth."

"Those are my handprints around your neck," Byron slurred thickly. He had his hands in his hair now, dragging at the strands in frustration.

Ronan could feel Byron's thoughts trying to push away from his own, but since he had no idea why or how they'd connected in his sleep he couldn't help. He wasn't even sure if he should. He wanted to hold him, but trying to project that feeling only seemed to make things worse.

"My teeth on your hands," Byron said. He was off the bed now, and backing toward the window. Every step between them made him harder to understand. "I hurt you. Tried to kill you, why aren't you screaming at me?"

"Do I sound like I could scream at you, even if I wanted to?" Ronan said irritably. He'd automatically stood to mirror Byron's movement and his knees were not tolerating the change of position. "You didn't do this."

"Stop saying that!"

"You *didn't*!" Ronan spat, his voice cracking on every other syllable as he continued, "do you *really* think this is the first time someone's tried to kill me? Bearing in mind the fact that we met in a hospital after I had my legs blown off in a fucking warzone? You were not in control of your body. Blaming you for this would be like blaming you for hitting me during an epileptic fit."

"I tried to chok–" Byron mumbled as Ronan followed him around the bed, putting himself between the door and his boyfriend.

"You didn't try any bloody thing at all! You were possessed! For fuck's sake Byron, if anyone is to blame it's your fucking parents for keeping you there all that time. Elspeth was using you."

"You barely even know me!" Byron shouted.

Behind the bed, the wall shook as someone in the next room thumped on it. The cops would show up if they didn't calm down soon.

"You're right," Ronan hissed, limping away and then turning back again. He was so stressed he couldn't work out what to do with himself. "But I'll tell you something I *do* know, Byron – I should be dead. You don't get injuries like mine in the middle of a covert operation and survive. I'm only here because of wishes, and luck, and magic. I am here for a reason, and I don't know for sure what that reason is, but I'm choosing to believe it's *you*."

He paused in his awkward pacing to look back at Byron but the man was just standing there with his mouth open.

"Do you really think I'm going to walk away from a love like this over something as petty as a possession? Considering you're already bloody psychic, and telekinetic, and you'll probably turn out to be a shapeshifter, or have fucking wings, or something." He was rambling now but he couldn't stop.

"What?" Byron looked like he'd lost the thread of the conversation a while ago.

"I get that you're worried about this," Ronan went on. "Yes, I'm smaller than you by about two inches and a hundred pounds, but I'm not helpless. You didn't – Elspeth didn't kill me. It tried and it failed. I can take care of myself. I got that thing out of you, then I got *you* out of *there*, six weeks off a double fucking knee replacement!" He winced and rubbed at the top of his thigh. "You are not a light man."

"Thanks."

"Oh, as if you don't work for it!"

"No. I mean it," Byron said quietly, sitting back down on the edge of bed. "I do. Thank you."

Ronan huffed and sat down next to him. Slowly Byron lowered his head onto his shoulder, being careful not to press against his neck.

"You lost your legs and somehow ended up with me? Do you know how crazy that sounds?"

"Almost as crazy as waking up your roommate because there's a werewolf at the door."

"Therianthrope," Byron corrected with a half-smile. Speech seemed to be getting easier for him with practice, even if his voice was still hard to understand. He gently traced the path of one knee surgery scar from the hem of Ronan's boxers down. "You'd have thought wishing for your legs back would mean getting complete limbs."

"I didn't specifically ask for my legs back. It was a strange wish," Ronan said with a shrug. "I think it worked the way it was meant to."

"What did you actually wish?"

Ronan laced their fingers together. "Not to be broken any more."

"What does that mean? Of the two of us you've always seemed like the one who had it together."

He could change the subject. He could laugh it off. He could mentally run away from the thought like he'd done so many times before.

"I don't do commitment," he said. "Or I didn't. I barely even dated by the end. It was all casual hook-ups and flings, never more than a few weeks at a time. If anyone so much as hinted at being fond of me, I'd end it. I've been scared of letting people get close for so long I barely noticed when it was happening with you."

"Why?"

His throat hurt like Elspeth's hands were trying to squeeze the life out of him again.

"I..." The words wouldn't come out of his mouth. Images of things he'd repressed for years began to rise from depths he didn't know his psyche possessed. Before they could fully surface Byron had moved to hug him tightly.

A wave of warmth flowed between them; the mental link seemingly unbroken. It was like all his emotions for Byron were being reflected back at him.

"I can't–"

"You don't have to tell me; everyone has bad shit in their past."

"It is in the past, I mean that. I'm never going to run away from you."

Byron nodded against his shoulder.

They sat in silence until the beep of a phone alarm drew Ronan back to his feet. "We need to decide what we're doing."

"Okay," Byron said. He stood too, then froze when he caught sight of his reflection in the bathroom mirror. "Oh, fuck."

Ronan watched him shamble across the room, his eyes inappropriately drawn to the shifting of Byron's thigh muscles for a moment before he decided to give him some privacy. There'd be time to admire his boyfriend when he wasn't still covered in dried blood.

He dressed slowly, cringing at the sensation of his clothes brushing over his various bruises.

Why hadn't he packed some shorts? Could he get away with being shirtless? Even with a shirt on, Byron usually looked half-naked since he cut half the fabric off most of his clothes, so no one would care if Ronan did the same, right?

He was fooling himself, next to Byron everyone would notice.

"Ronan?" Byron called from the bathroom. "Speaking of broken – why is the coffee machine in pieces?"

"I needed to sterilize water to clean your face, and there was no kettle."

"Okay, and why are there sugar packets all over the counter?"

"Don't touch those," he said, wandering over to find Byron standing naked with one foot in the shower cubicle. He must have gotten distracted.

Ronan scooped up the packets before the humidity from the shower made them dissolve. "I tried these before I resorted to the metal symbols. It's edible tapioca paper made with holy water, filled with exorcised salt, white oak, clove, garlic, and a trace amount of silver. Didn't stop Elspeth, but hurt enough to make it scream and open your mouth."

Byron shivered and turned away.

"Why are those a thing you have?"

"I got suspicious about the things you were saying about the summer house. Think of these as 'universal bad thing repellent.'"

The shower door closed without any further comment.

12

BYRON'S PHONE RANG SHORTLY AFTER THEY JOINED THE INTERSTATE, heading towards Philadelphia, where Byron had found a dentist who could see him in an emergency. It was two hours in the wrong direction, but right now Ronan would take any excuse to put more road between them and the thing in the summer house.

They'd already texted Darcey and asked her to cover for them. He'd work out what to do about the ruined bedroom while he was waiting for Byron to be treated.

"It's Uncle Mac," Byron said in surprise as he peered at the phone in his hand. Before Ronan could say anything about the caller, he'd hit the answer button. "Hey, you're on speakerphone."

"Oh, thank god you're okay."

They shared a look but neither of them felt like correcting him. Mac sounded so relieved that Ronan felt a pang of guilt for the state he'd had to leave Byron's room in – he'd taken the bloody sheets from the bed but there had been far more damage than he'd had time to clean up.

"Why, what's up?" Byron asked as clearly as he could, despite the mess that was his tongue.

"There was, uh, a problem last night...something got into the house."

Again, they glanced at each other. Mac was speaking like every word was being physically dragged out of him. Had someone been hurt? Had the thing that got into Byron managed to possess someone else after they left?

"What happened?"

"Your dad thinks it was a mountain lion..."

"There aren't any mountain lions in the Hamptons!" Byron scoffed. Ronan flicked his elbow for interrupting.

"Darcey said she saw a big dog running away into the trees behind your house," Mac went on. "It, uh, it got into the kitchens and ate everything your mom had ordered for the party. Trashed the place – downstairs and your room for some reason – then disappeared."

"Huh. Weird."

Ronan wished he wasn't driving so he could give Byron the long drawn-out look of disappointment he deserved.

"A big dog?" he asked, loudly enough for the phone's mic to catch his voice. "Mac...where did you wake up this morning?"

There was a pregnant pause so drawn out that the pause had given birth to five pause puppies before the man on the phone finally mumbled, "Underneath someone's boathouse on the north shore."

"Naked?"

"...Yeah."

"Why were yo–" Byron began, but Ronan flicked him again.

"Remember the hospital?" he prompted, and made a clawing motion with his hand. To Mac he said, "I bet you had a fun time getting back to the house then."

"It was early, and only about four miles through a lot of backyards. Half the yards out here are bigger than the town I grew up in. It wasn't too difficult not to be seen." Mac had almost been laughing for a second before his tone turned somber again. "But then I got back to the house and saw the mess. Ben – Byron, sorry – why was there blood up the walls in your room? I cleaned it before your mom woke up, but..."

His voice cracked and Ronan felt another wave of guilt that he hadn't had time to deal with it all himself.

"I thought I'd eaten you."

"Okay," Byron said, "that's wildly underestimating the amount of blood a human bo–"

This time Ronan outright slapped Byron's arm.

"For fuck's sake! Mac, I'm so sorry you thought that. We're both fine. We just...we just had some weirdness, like your weirdness. Everything's fine, but I'm taking Byron to an emergency dentist right now to get things sorted out. Can you tell his parents...something?"

He glanced at Byron for some input but he'd crossed his arms in a very childish pout.

"I already said you'd had to go back to D.C. for medical reasons," Mac said sheepishly.

Byron's frown deepened. "You thought you might have *eaten* us and you immediately jumped to lying about where we were?"

"I called you, didn't I? I would have gone and looked for you if you hadn't answered the phone!"

Ronan had to resist the urge to rub his forehead in frustration – the Fury didn't have power steering and he didn't trust his driving enough to take a hand off the wheel for as long as it would take to scrub away his frustration.

"Mac, thank you; Byron, stop it. Would you rather he'd told your mother that you were missing and there was blood everywhere? I've only met her once and she already thinks I'm some kind of pervert, I don't need her thinking I'm a violent psychopath, too."

"But, Ronan, you are a pervert."

"Byron!"

His companion laughed heartily for a second then grabbed his own jaw with a hiss of pain. Ronan had no sympathy.

"Aww come on, kid, I used to change your diapers," Mac protested, "I don't need to hear that kinda detail about your love life."

"Any idea why you changed?" Ronan asked, trying to steer the conversation back onto the slightly safer topic of Byron's uncle being some kind of shapeshifting monster.

"I never know why it happens, I told you that." The speed of Mac's snap reply suggested a habitual unwillingness to think about the question.

Ronan had seen that kind of reaction before from younger soldiers who didn't want to face the reasons behind their anger management or impulse control issues. Over time it had a habit of calcifying into a refusal to be introspective about anything. He could understand why a man in his sixties would cling to that kind of ignorance, but it wasn't healthy.

He pressed on, "I know, but yesterday – did you do something you wouldn't normally do, or eat something you wouldn't normally eat?"

157

"Well, I sure as shit don't eat the kind of fancy food Gianna makes while I'm on the road, but it was all things I've eaten before."

"Yeah, I don't think lycanthropy is a known side effect of food allergies," Byron added sarcastically. "I'm pretty sure that'd end up on the news – 'kid with peanut allergy sprouts hair and fangs after being offered nuts on transatlantic flight, more on this story at eleven'."

"No, but mysterious deaths happen every day, who's to say it would ever get out? 'Kid transforms, attacks pilots, plane crashes into the ocean leaving no evidence' is much more likely than it getting onto the news."

"That's not a comforting image," Mac grumbled.

"Exactly! I'm not saying you've ever actually killed anyone, but wouldn't you rather know what's going on?"

From the corner of his eye he could see the worried look on Byron's face. He shouldn't have brought up that possibility even if he'd just been building on Byron's own joke – they had no idea how often Mac changed or what happened when he did. He still travelled alone with David once in a while. Just because Byron didn't get along with his parents didn't mean he wanted to think about his uncle accidentally killing his father.

The only response Mac gave was a thoughtful grumble.

"It's not like this happens every day, right? There must be something," Byron said, in what would have been a wheedling tone if his voice weren't so low.

Mac mumbled an 'I'll think about it,' apparently persuaded by something in the way Byron spoke. Maybe he sounded like the child Mac used to know.

"Gimme some time, Ben, I'll call you back."

Byron dropped his phone on the seat when the call disconnected, and slumped back. He suddenly looked even more exhausted than before, which was saying something, given how bad he'd looked when he first woke up.

Confident that the road would be straight for a little while, Ronan finally let go of the wheel for long enough to squeeze his hand. There wasn't much else he could do right now.

It seemed that Byron had some kind of reaction to the dental anesthetic –

he'd fallen asleep almost as soon as they got back into the car, only waking briefly at loud noises or sudden maneuvers. Oddly enough, Ronan didn't mind the quiet after a while. It was pleasant to listen to the engine and the sound of Byron's breathing.

The Fury took some getting used to, though fortunately Ronan had driven enough finicky military vehicles in his time that he soon adapted to the weight of the steering. There wasn't much in the way of suspension, so his knees would hate him in the morning, but once they were on the interstate the ride wasn't so bad. He could see why Byron loved the car; it was like driving inside your own personal home.

Where was his home?

At no point since he'd woken up in the hospital had he thought about going back to England. His career was over. His family was just his father and grandfather – neither of whom had ever sparked much familial feeling in his heart. What else did he have?

Another ten miles had passed beneath the wheels before he came to the conclusion that there was nothing else.

He'd never owned a place of his own. All his life he'd gone where other people told him to go.

Beside him Byron snuffled in his sleep, the leather of the bench seat creaking under him as he shifted position.

The car was probably wide enough to lay across the seats, even if they were both slightly too tall to do so comfortably. Had Byron ever mentioned sleeping in the car when he told Ronan about finding it? Ronan couldn't remember.

It must be possible. Even if it wasn't, the motels here weren't all that expensive.

The idea was sneaking up on him in stages, and he daren't look at it too directly in case it ran away from him like a frightened animal, but he could feel the edges of it.

He ran his thumbs over the warm texture of the steering wheel, following the line of the leather tape as it wound around the metal.

The freeway he was heading towards went all the way to Florida.

Other roads went to other places.

He laughed to himself at that ridiculous thought. All roads went somewhere. He was being melodramatic.

Still, he could go anywhere. If he wanted.

They'd had a hard night, and a worse morning, but after the last few months Ronan had a sense of lightness he never thought he'd get to experience again.

His military career was over.

He'd known that since he first woke in the hospital, but sitting here – at the traffic light, in a car twice his age, looking at the boyfriend he felt like he had been with forever – Ronan realized he didn't care anymore. That had been a different life, for a different person.

Behind them someone honked.

The light had changed.

"Everything okay?" Byron mumbled thickly as they moved off, one hand idly flipping the bird at the truck overtaking them.

The dentist had said his voice would be messed up for a while, though he would recover completely given time. Ronan didn't want to go too long without hearing him speak in that deep rumble of his.

"Yeah," he said. "Just thinking."

"About what?"

"Home."

"The apartment? Or England?"

Whether the question was being asked with fear Ronan couldn't tell around the slurring, but he placed a hand on Byron's knee all the same.

"Nothing that specific." Ronan made a face that he hoped would convey his meaning – he couldn't really shrug while driving a car as old and heavy as the Fury. "Well, in terms of map references anyway."

"Did you get into my meds?" Byron leaned across the wide bench seat to peer at him suspiciously. "Because that makes no sense. Unless I'm still asleep. My dreams never make sense. Especially that one with the lobster…"

"I'm pretty sure we're awake. If I was asleep, you'd either look much better or much worse than you do now."

Byron tried to stick his tongue out, but hissed at the pain instead. Ronan squeezed his knee.

"I meant I wasn't thinking about one particular place as home," he said, "more the entire concept. Some people would say your parents' house was home–"

"I wouldn't," Byron said darkly.

Nothing about the blank white walls of Byron's childhood bedroom would have screamed 'home' to Ronan's mind, and that was even before one considered the literal demon in the backyard.

"No," he said slowly, "me neither. But some people say home is where you grew up. My father's been in England since he was five and he still talks about going home to Limerick."

"What do you think?"

"I used to think the army was my home," Ronan said. There was far less regret in his voice than he expected. "I never owned a house of my own – I was always in barracks. Before that I was at boarding school. I can't say that the places I got sent over the summers would ever count as home."

"Hmm, same. When I got my first place, I thought it'd change my life. You know, a home of your own. Wasn't until I found this car that I had any idea what that phrase actually meant." Byron leaned forward to pet the dashboard like any other person would have stroked the side of their favorite dog.

"But you still got your apartment in D.C.?"

A vague shrug. "Gianna arranged all of that. She wanted more stability for me. At the time it seemed like a good compromise. A way towards being a proper adult."

Ronan couldn't help raising his eyebrows at that. Despite his muscular build it was hard to see Byron as a real grown-up under all the tattoos and the hair dye, but even harder to imagine him without them. He tried to picture Byron in a sensible suit with his hair neatly brushed. His brain just glitched out.

By the side of the road a sign announced that they were approaching I-95 – the interstate that ran the whole length of the eastern seaboard.

By going to the dentist Byron chose, he'd ended up putting three hours of road between them and his childhood home. Now it was a question of whether they drove all that way back, or if they just headed home to the apartment in D.C. instead.

Going back to his parent's house would mean explaining what happened last night. Mac had cleaned everything up and given them an excuse to leave. That didn't mean they had to stay away, but there was still the matter of Byron's face and Ronan's neck.

They would probably be safer letting Byron's parents be upset about the sudden departure than frightening them with new injuries.

Either way it wasn't Ronan's choice to make. He turned to Byron.

"Where do you want to go?"

"I don't want to go back there."

"Okay." There wasn't anything else he needed to say.

By the time they made it home Ronan felt as if he'd been on a weeklong survival exercise rather than spending a few hours driving. Technically he probably shouldn't have been behind the wheel at all, but first adrenaline and then necessity had put him there. His knees would be telling him about it for days.

Seeing his discomfort, Byron had tried to carry him up the stairs out of the parking garage, but Ronan didn't trust that the medication had quite worn off, so he'd insisted on using the elevator.

When they were alone in there Byron had come in for a kiss, as he always did.

Sadly, he'd forgotten the stitches and lingering pain from his recent dental repairs – Ronan had ended up with a whimpering boyfriend and scraps of cotton wool between his teeth.

On that unhappy note they'd both agreed to retreat to bed – and sleep – until the morning could bring more comfortable circumstances.

Instead, the morning brought Mac to their door.

Ronan was sorely tempted not to answer. He'd woken up with his arm around a thick warm chest, and his nose buried in the coconut-scented, over-styled locks of Byron's hair. He wanted to stay there forever, or at least for the rest of the week. Certain parts of his anatomy were firmly in agreement, as it were.

He smiled at his own terrible pun, then sighed when Mac shouted at them from the hallway again.

No rest for the wicked, then.

Fortunately, this time he had the chance to put on some underwear and a robe before he answered the door. Enough members of Byron's family had seen more than he ever wanted them to see. No need to traumatize anyone with morning wood.

For some reason Mac had brought them a fruit basket.

The unexpected gift was huge, probably about four feet tall and god only knew how many pounds. There were fruits in there Ronan didn't even recognize. Mac was just a pair of eyes and a beat-up trucker's cap peering around a mass of groceries.

"Hi, can I come in?" Mac said, stepping forward before Ronan could answer. "I had an idea."

There was no way Ronan could resist the sheer volume of fruit without toppling Mac backwards out into the hall, so he stepped aside. Whatever his idea was, it would no doubt be better explained behind closed doors. Ronan had barely seen the neighbors, but he knew conversations about shapeshifters wouldn't go down well with the general eavesdropping population.

"Oh, hey, cool gift, thanks!" Byron said as he appeared from nowhere – not to help, but to try to extract a peach from the middle of the pile. It looked like a load-bearing peach so Ronan dragged him back before they ended up with a floor covered in ruined produce.

Speaking of peaches, Byron had not bothered to get dressed beyond a pair of retro boxers that left very little to the imagination.

"As much as I admire the view, please go and put some clothes on," Ronan murmured. "I think Mac will be here for a while."

"Sorry," Mac said as Byron stomped away to the bedroom, "I didn't think you boys would still be asleep at four in the afternoon."

Ronan opened his mouth to argue that it couldn't possibly be that late, but his body immediately started reporting that it had the horrible sort of dehydration headache that came with twenty hours of uninterrupted sleep. Before he could formulate any kind of dignified excuse, Mac had put the basket down and stepped into his personal space.

Despite the height difference Ronan suddenly felt like he was fifteen years old and staring his father down after an argument.

"What happened to his mouth?" Mac asked in a hiss that wasn't entirely accusing. He glanced down and frowned. "What happened to your neck?"

Even though the damage was already done, Ronan couldn't stop the instinctive impulse to pull the collar of his robe a little higher, which only drew attention to his hands. The bruises around the bite marks had blossomed to a dark purple that seemed especially stark against his skin's natural pallor. He didn't want to know what his neck looked like right now.

"It's not entirely my story to tell, but it's similar to your situation. In a way. Byron tells me that he was a 'problem child' when he was young, did you ever experience that side of him?"

Mac's lips twisted together for a moment before he nodded, clearly weighing up how much to say. His expression had shifted from accusing to a pitying kind of concern much faster than Ronan would like.

Ronan decided to take the pressure off him. "There's an unusual explanation for his behavior," he said, "but it's up to him if he feels comfortable sharing it. Just know that we're both adults, and we're both going to be fine. Not all that long ago, I was shot out of the sky and nearly bled to death – I can look after myself."

He almost jumped when Byron's arm slipped around his waist, but years of looking dignified in front of other soldiers kept his feet on the ground.

"You don't have to," Byron said, in what would have been a romantic moment if Ronan hadn't immediately ruined it by saying over him–

"How the hell did you get dressed that quickly?"

The frustration of all those weeks of waiting forty minutes to get into their hospital suite bathroom every morning had bubbled to the surface and taken control of his mouth.

"I don't have to do my hair for Uncle Mac," Byron shrugged. "He knows what I look like."

"And yet you were doing it for nurses you'd literally never see again?"

Byron gave him an awkward smile despite the lingering swelling around his mouth.

"No, that was for you."

Caught somewhere between irritation and flattery, Ronan opted to escape the entire conversation to regroup.

"I'm gonna go find some clothes," he said as he all but fled the room. If he couldn't stop happily smiling to himself while he dressed, then no one needed to know.

"Mac's got a really good idea to solve The Mystery of The Giant Wolf-Thing," Byron said, when Ronan finally returned in jeans and a shirt buttoned up over his bruises.

Ronan laughed. He'd taken his pain medication as soon as he returned to their room and it was already improving his spirits.

"How do you manage to pronounce capital letters like that?"

With hands spread wide like a ringmaster, Byron cried "showmanship!"

Clearly, he was feeling a lot better as well.

Byron gestured to where Mac was sitting at the table with the fruit neatly laid out in front of him.

"Let us begin."

Ronan held up a hand of his own, "Ah, no, let us *carefully* discuss the plan first! Mac?"

"I know doctors say you should eat five a day, but it's hard to get fresh fruit and vegetables out on the road, especially when the truck stops have got more appealing things on offer–"

"Like waffles."

"Yeah, thanks Byron, like waffles, and pie, and–"

"You can put fruit on waffles. Or in pie."

Ronan stepped around behind Byron's chair and – gently – covered his mouth. Mac was looking sheepish enough without the constant interruptions.

"Sorry about him, go on."

"Anyway, I was saying – I don't usually get fresh fruit when I'm out on the road these days. It was different when I was working with your dad," Mac nodded to Byron, referencing David's murky past, "in those countries there were stalls in every village. It was harder to get processed food than fresh back in those days."

"What work were you doing?" Ronan asked.

"Logistics."

Somehow Mac managed to put significantly more meaning into that word than it ever usually contained, without actually telling him anything at all.

"Logistics?"

Mac just gave them a blank look.

"He means smuggling," Byron said.

"Ah, *Logistics*. And did you ever transform while you were doing that kind of work?"

"Yeah. Not often though. Well, I *think* I changed. To be fair, there were a few reasons a guy might have woken up naked in a field back then," Mac shot Byron an apologetic smile as he made a smoking gesture.

"Do you remember anything about the locations where you changed?"

Mac counted out the answer on his fingers. "Mostly in Europe, a few times in Canada, never in Asia, once in South America."

"And I'm guessing you brought fruit because you think that might be the cause?" Ronan asked. He'd decided Byron could probably be trusted to be sensible by now, and had walked around the table to study the selection on offer.

"Like I said – I don't eat fresh fruit very often. When I was... doing surveillance at the hospital–"

"Spying on me."

"Yeah, spying on you," Mac said with a shrug. "Also, stealing from you. Technically. I got hungry and the vending machine was broken, so I stole the fruit cups from your dinner trays."

While Byron looked inexplicably scandalized – his uncle had just admitted to being a smuggler after all – Ronan couldn't help but laugh.

"That explains the first incident, but are you really saying that after transforming in the hospital the first time you did it again on another day and didn't make the connection?"

Mac had the decency to look a little bit sheepish at that.

"Well," Ronan said, poking at some of the fruit, "I think we can rule some of these out immediately. Or save them until last. I'm not even sure what this one is..."

Byron took the pink and spiky object from him with a condescending smile.

"Never seen pitaya before? Dragon fruit?"

There was no point pretending to be more cultured than he was. "Can't say that I have. I don't think lychees are common in hospital food either. Or star fruit. Besides, you said transformations happened mostly here and in Europe. So, we start with foods that match those areas."

"Okay."

"Wait!"

Mac had the apple almost in his mouth when Ronan grabbed his arm and pulled it away.

"We can't do this in the apartment," he said.

"Why not?" Byron asked.

"You barricaded our door when he was just in the hospital's hallway! Where are we supposed to hide in here if he changes? The door isn't even locked, what if he runs off into the street in monster form? Or jumps off the balcony?"

"But we know it's him now, Mac would never hurt us."

Ronan rubbed his throat, deliberately rearranging the collar that was mostly covering his bruises.

"Wouldn't he?"

Byron made a face, but he got the point.

"I'm going to start now, okay?" Mac's voice was muffled as he tried to shout through the back doors of the refrigerated truck.

It hadn't been their first choice – they'd tried to find an armored car, or a prisoner transport van, but there was no way to borrow those on short notice without arousing a lot of suspicion. Although as a long-haul truck driver, it made some sense that Mac might need to borrow a refrigerated unit to replace one that had broken down.

The external locks looked strong enough for their purposes. Or rather, Ronan hoped they were strong enough.

No part of this seemed like a good idea any more.

"Okay, remember to say what you're eating!" Ronan called back, trying not to feel terribly conspicuous.

The truck was parked in the abandoned lot of a long since demolished video rental store, about an hour and a half outside the city. It was mostly hidden from the road by the weeds that grew up through the cracked asphalt, but Ronan found it hard to believe that no one would notice Byron.

He was wearing galaxy print leggings, for god's sake.

"Banana!" Came the first shout, then a pause. "Nothing! Apple... Nothing... Orange... Nothing..."

"You know," Byron said conversationally, while Ronan jotted down the results. "We never actually asked how long it takes between eating and transforming–"

"Oh, fuck. Mac! Stop!" Ronan put his head in his hands and sighed. How had he not thought of that?

"Whut?"

"If it happened immediately, he'd know, wouldn't he?" Ronan said, mostly to himself. "I can't believe I did that. Fuck. If he transforms now it could be any of the first three, so we'd have to repeat the test. If he doesn't, then we'll have wasted the whole night."

"Dude, just ask him! It might not be that bad. I mean, maybe he's just really unobservant."

Ronan resisted the urge to comment that not paying attention to strange things appeared to be a Williams family trait.

Byron banged on the side of the truck. "Hey, Mac, how long does it usually take to transform?"

"I dunno, I fall asleep and then – boom! Werewolf."

"Well, in that case, you're gonna have to go to sleep."

"Okay, can do." Mac's reply was casual enough, which hopefully meant he'd developed that wonderful life skill of being able to sleep anywhere. If not, it was going to be a very long night.

There were some shuffling noises from inside the truck. Then silence.

"So, what do we do now?" Byron asked, looking around the overgrown lot as if something interesting would appear from the undergrowth.

"Wait."

"We could make out. While we're waiting."

Ronan stared at him. Was there a diplomatic way to say 'I'm thirty-five years old, we're standing in the middle of a wasteland, waiting to find out what makes your 'uncle' a monster – this isn't the time or the place'? The situation wasn't helped by the fact that he actually wouldn't mind kissing him right now.

It wasn't *appropriate*, but Byron did look good in those leggings, and the setting sun was really highlighting the curve of his arms. Plus, it was getting chilly.

They'd missed out on some quality snuggling time when Mac so rudely got them out of bed. No one would blame them for–

There was a horrible noise.

If Ronan was asked to describe the sound later, he would have said it was almost exactly like several pounds of corned beef being dropped into a vacuum cleaner. Why he knew what that scenario would sound like he couldn't say, but that was definitely what he was hearing.

"What the hell is that?" he asked. He almost had to shout to be heard.

The noise reverberated for several seconds, seemingly coming from everywhere at once, before it tapered off into silence again.

Byron pointed silently to the truck.

"Shit!" Ronan cried. "He transformed already? Bloody hell, he really doesn't eat much fruit if something as common as banana or orange made him change."

The sound started again and Ronan finally noticed the grin on Byron's face.

"He's snoring."

"I don't believe you, that's not a human noise."

"Trust me," Byron laughed, "I travelled with him and my dad a couple of times a year as a kid. He's always sounded like that."

"He's definitely not related to you by genetics, is he?" Ronan was pretty sure he wasn't, but he felt the need to check.

Byron shook his head. "No, he's just a close-family-friend kind of uncle. Why? Do you think being a huge monster is a genetic trait?"

"No, I was just thinking that if that kind of snoring was going to be in our future, I might have to consider sewing my own ears closed."

For some reason that made Byron blush. It was hard to see the color change in the fading light, but the way he dipped his head, as if a man his size could ever be shy, was just adorable.

"What?" Ronan asked, stepping closer to make eye contact.

"I just..." Byron dragged him into an unexpected bear hug. "I'm so happy you didn't jump straight to dumping me."

"I stayed through you being possessed by a demon, I'm not going to break up with you just because you might start making more noise than the entire army of hell!"

Ronan had to shout the last few words to be heard over the next round of snoring.

He could feel Byron laughing against his hair. Well, he hoped he was laughing. Either way, he wrapped his arms around Byron's hips and let himself be held for a while. They had nothing better to do.

They stood there for several minutes, but the tone and rhythm of the sound didn't change.

"We're gonna have to wake him up, we can't just wait forever."

Without replying or letting go, Byron slammed one fist into the side of the truck, startling half a dozen crows from a nearby tree with the resounding bang.

"Whuzzat?" they heard Mac grumble from inside the truck.

"Still human?"

"Looks like it!" he said, after a worryingly long pause.

Byron and Ronan shared a look – it shouldn't be that hard to tell what species you were, but it was probably as good an answer as they were doing to get.

"Okay," Ronan called, "eat the next fruit, and try to go back to sleep."

"Right! This one's a strawberry!"

As far as Ronan could tell Mac hadn't even gotten up from wherever he was sleeping. After he confirmed the kind of fruit he was eating, there was no sound until the snoring started again.

"How long do we let him sleep this time?" Byron asked.

He still had one arm around Ronan's shoulders to hold him against his chest, while his other hand was resting against the side of the truck. While they were waiting, the last of the sunset had drained from the sky – somehow his muscles looked even better in the moonlight.

Ronan was very tempted to return to his earlier suggestion.

"Hmmm..." he said, with a coy smile.

Byron smiled back, and absently tapped his fingertips against the truck.

Whatever he said in reply was completely drowned out by a terrible snarling noise and something massive slamming into the wall of the truck from the inside.

They both jumped back, tangling their feet in the process to end up laid in a heap on the broken asphalt. Ronan was mostly on top. Byron tightened his arms to keep him there.

"Oh, now, this is a good way to spend our time," Byron laughed.

"So, you're not concerned that *strawberries* just changed your uncle into a giant monster?"

"No?" Byron gave as close to a shrug as he could, mostly pinned as he was under Ronan's weight. "I mean, it sucks, but at least we know now. And we can't do anything about it until sunrise. The locks seem to be holding, and there's plenty of food in there–"

As if on cue, the sound of snarling changed to a munching, crunching noise that was somehow louder than any of the other noises had been.

"Pineapple? Or grapefruit?"

"I was going to guess watermelon, to be honest."

Byron shook his head. "Nah, I dropped one of those from a third-floor window onto a bear trap once, it would sound wetter."

"You can't just say something like that without the rest of the story! Tell me more."

Laying on the asphalt was going to get unpleasant eventually, but Byron was warm and surprisingly comfortable. Like he'd said, they had nothing better to do. So, Ronan let his head rest on Byron's shoulder and listened to the tale of one especially mad summer, while beside them the truck occasionally rocked on its suspension.

Mac seemed to be demolishing that fruit basket.

Ronan hoped there wouldn't be a cleaning bill at the end of this.

13

"THAT WAS FUN!" BYRON SAID CHEERFULLY, AS HE GAVE ONE LAST wave at the back of Mac's car before it made a turn and disappeared among the heavy traffic.

Ronan yawned.

He didn't disagree, not entirely, but he was wiped out.

They'd spent most of the night on the ground, sharing mostly funny stories from their lives, and just generally enjoying each other's company until they both dozed off. It had been a surprisingly relaxing night given what was in the truck beside them.

Sadly, the morning had brought stiff, aching limbs from the cold ground, as well pain from the injuries that were still supposed to be healing. Ronan could already picture the disapproving look his physiotherapist would give him if he ever admitted to sleeping in a parking lot. His knees were voicing their displeasure with every awkward step he took.

He should have taken his crutches with him.

In terms of 'fun,' he certainly wouldn't have used that word to describe the scene they'd found inside the truck when it finally felt safe to open the back doors.

Mac had transformed as soon as he was fully exposed to sunlight, but for a moment he'd looked like a dog that had fallen into a vat at a pudding factory, only nine feet tall and utterly terrifying.

Then he'd looked exactly the same except for the part where he was a naked middle-aged man.

There had been fruit chunks caught in his body hair.

Every part of his body hair.

Ronan hadn't meant to look, but the human mind is not kind,

and now he'd probably never get that image out of his head again.

There was also fruit on every single surface of the truck, but he'd barely noticed that until Byron pointed out that they'd have to clean it all before they returned it.

In the end they'd gone to a jet washing place, where they'd paid the owner a hundred dollars to let them do the job themselves – and not comment on the very hirsute man they were hosing down as well. Frankly, he was amazed no one called the police on them.

Now the truck was returned, Mac was gone, and they were exhausted.

His stomach rumbled. When the hell had he last eaten?

"Breakfast? Or bed?" Byron asked. "Are you hungry? Because I know–"

"Don't."

" –where we can get a fruit salad."

"I hate you," Ronan groaned. "I'm never going to be able to look at fruit again. Urgh, I'm exhausted, but if I lay down now, I'll sleep for a week. Is there somewhere local we can get food? Preferably something carb-based, and fruit-free."

"Absolutely. Follow me."

Half a dozen waffles is too many for a normal human being.

It shouldn't be possible to measure the height of a person's breakfast in feet and inches.

When Byron ordered his 'usual,' Ronan hadn't expected the waitress to bring out a food challenge. Of course, there had been the 'whole roast chicken at 3am' incident in the hospital, but he could more or less understand that from a protein perspective. Byron had to feed those muscles somehow. Three adults worth of carbohydrates though – that didn't seem like a wise choice.

Ronan tried not to make eye contact with the waitress as she refilled his coffee. He didn't want to know what her facial expression was going to be.

His own Danishes looked comically small in comparison, and he already knew he wouldn't be able to finish them.

"You okay?" Byron asked, once they were alone.

There was no kind way to say 'I'm embarrassed by your breakfast selection' so Ronan settled for "Yeah."

"Can you tell me the truth for a minute?"

He wasn't sure why Byron might doubt him, but he could play along. "About what?"

"What do you want to do?"

"What, this afternoon?" The question made no sense. "Shower, I guess. Sleep. Sleep some more. Why?"

"No, I mean..." Byron turned his face away so his expression was mostly hidden by his hair. The green highlights made the brown of his eyes seem warmer. "What do you want to do in general? You've been staying with me to be near the treatment facilities–"

Ronan reached out across the table to cover his hand. Byron's knuckles had turned white where he was gripping the fork too tightly.

"Is that really what you think of me? I'm staying with you because I want to, because–" He sighed.

The L-word had almost made it past his lips. Again. It had slipped out once already, during the argument in the motel room. He wanted to say it, but if Byron could still doubt him after the incident with Elspeth, well... perhaps he hadn't heard.

It wouldn't have been the first time that Byron had failed to notice something Ronan thought was obvious.

"I keep telling you how much I like you," Ronan went on when Byron failed to look up. "I hope I've been showing it too. Do you really think someone who was using you for accommodation would stay through the whole possession thing? Or finding out why your uncle turns into a monster? I'm here because I want to be."

"How long are you going to want to be here though?" Although his fingers had relaxed a little, Byron still didn't meet his eye. "You told me you don't do long-term relationships. Not with 'humans' anyway."

Byron said the word 'human' like it was both a slur and a label he didn't entirely believe applied to himself.

"As soon as you're back on your feet and not broken anymore – why would you stick around with me?" Byron muttered.

"Hey, where is all this coming from?" Ronan felt sick to his stomach, and he was sure it was showing on his face. He'd never meant for Byron to take any of the things he said about being broken that way.

"Just now, you looked like you were embarrassed to be seen with me–"

"Whoa, no, that's..." He sighed. He wanted to put his head onto the table in despair, but eye contact seemed more important right now. "Look, you have enough food in front of you to feed a family of four for a week. That's all. Sometimes you're going to do things that make me cringe, and maybe I'll embarrass you too. It's never going to be a reason for me to break up with you."

Byron's shoulders slumped a little as some of the tension drained away.

"Okay, I'm sorry. I get that. I guess I panicked. Maybe I'm just hungry."

He reached for the stack of waffles as if he was going to pick one up with his bare hands.

Ronan shook his head.

After a moment Byron sheepishly grabbed the utensils to cut up his food like a civilized person.

"I'm here for the long haul," Ronan said. To his surprise he meant it. "I know what I told you before, about my past relationships, but...that was then. This is now. Physically healing is a process with an end. I don't think emotional healing works the same way. I don't expect to wake up one day and say 'I'm all better now, bye.'"

"Are you ever going to tell me what happened?"

"One day, maybe." Ronan let his gaze drift back to his plate. He didn't feel like eating anymore. "It's not that I don't trust you with the information, I don't trust myself to share it yet."

At the edge of his vision, he saw Byron nod his head a little.

"So, what *do* you want to do with your life?" Byron asked. "If you stay with me, I mean. Are you going to get a job here?"

To be fair, Ronan hadn't really thought about that. Since he'd woke up, any thoughts of the future had been focused on his recovery. That was what the army liaison had told him to do – after a lifetime of following orders, he'd done as he was told.

From the age of five years old he'd dreamed of being a paratrooper. Everything he'd done since then had been focused on working towards achieving and maintaining that goal. He had no idea how to transfer that to anything else. He had skills that would be valuable in a workplace – leadership skills and the like – but which industry, and at what level, was a mystery to him.

A few months ago, he'd been entirely responsible for life and death situations. He tried to imagine himself in a suit and tie, managing a bunch of clerks, and talking about the Johnson Report like it actually mattered.

He couldn't see it.

What could he see then?

Reaching across the table, Ronan took hold of Byron's hand again.

Byron smiled at him, a little brighter this time despite the slice of waffle he was still chewing.

"Do you remember what I said back at the motel?" Ronan asked, wondering if he was about to make a mistake. When Byron frowned and shook his head, Ronan added, "Let me show you then."

It was difficult to separate the worry and fear they'd both felt in that moment from the memory of the words but Ronan hoped that Byron would understand what he was trying to tell him.

As he replayed the memory of his own voice saying 'do you really think I'm going to walk away from a love like this over something as petty as a possession?' Ronan tried to fill his mind with the affection that had driven his accidental declaration. It was easier than he had expected.

This time when Byron smiled, it wasn't the sardonic persona-maintaining smile he usually gave, but something wide and genuine, all teeth and crinkled eyes. In Ronan's mind the affection intensified like sunlight reflecting off a mirror.

Byron's hand flexed under his fingertips. Something about the ridges of his knuckles reminded Ronan of the texture of the Fury's steering wheel.

"I don't have any career plans right now," Ronan said. "It's not the time yet to make those kinds of choices. I have savings, I can be comfortable for a good chunk of time before I need to make any decisions. Do you know what I *do* see myself doing? Spending time with you. Really getting to know you. Maybe having some more adventures."

"Like what?"

"You told me you travelled a lot when you first ran away from your parents. You also told me that the car feels like home. Now it's sitting in a parking garage without even the sun on its paintwork. Don't you think it deserves to have a little more fun than that?" Ronan winked. The more he thought about it, the more options for entertainment the car offered. "We could probably sleep in there. Keep each other warm."

"Mmmm, good point." Byron's expression turned lascivious at the hint, then immediately faded.

Releasing his grip on Ronan's hand, Byron rubbed at the still livid scar that cut through his shoulder tattoos and the muscle underneath.

"I can't drive for very long yet," he said sadly. "I probably shouldn't have even gone as far as my parents' house. I'm still getting tingling sensations now and I've slept since then."

Ronan felt a pang of guilt and tried to bury it under a bite of his Danish.

"Sorry," he said around the pastry. "I can't say I was very gentle getting you out of your parents' house. I had to drag you down a flight of stairs. We should probably get you checked out again. Besides, I don't think any of what we've had over the last few days counts as real sleep."

Byron nodded. His other injuries from that night had almost been forgotten in the rush to deal with his mouth; Ronan had certainly done his best to forget his own.

"We're both a mess," Ronan added quietly, not wanting to make Byron feel guilty as well. "I probably shouldn't drive for very long either. I know we still have treatments to get through, but we could break up the pain with a day trip or two..."

His musings were cut off by a more serious consideration.

"Ronan, what about Elspeth?"

That was a question that had been weighing on the back of his mind ever since he hauled Byron into that motel room. He didn't have a good answer.

"Has it ever affected anyone else in the family? As far as you know?"

Byron stabbed a waffle viciously with his fork, partially demolishing the remaining half of the stack. Ronan still didn't know where he was putting it all. Most of the time he didn't even notice him actively eating.

"I don't think so. It's hard to know what's happening when I'm not there, but I don't think it has ever directly influenced my parents. Just made them miserable through me." Another stab of his fork. "When I'm not there they always seem to be happy. I don't want things to get that bad for us as well."

"Fuck that," Ronan said baldly. "That evil thing has no power over me."

"So, what do we do?"

"Have you ever heard the phrase 'discretion is the better part of valor'?"

Byron shook his head.

"Basically, it means – pick your battles; know what you're going into; don't be a pig-headed idiot who gets themselves killed because they were underprepared." Ronan leaned forward and stole a chunk of waffle from Byron's plate. "I put it to you that we are both injured. We're both tired. We only have a vague idea of what that thing is, and currently it doesn't seem to be threatening anyone else."

"Mmhmm," Byron mumbled with a full mouth, nodding on every point.

"Going in there right now would be a disaster. We're not ready. Personally, I think we should put this on the back burner until we have everything together, and we're both fighting fit." Ronan didn't mention that he had no idea when that would be, or, in his case, if it would ever happen at all – it would take months for his legs to settle into their final condition. They might never be perfect.

"So, we relax–"

"Convalesce."

Based on Byron's expression he didn't recognize that word, but he soldiered on, regardless.

"So, we do that," he said, "and we – what? Head out the door and just wander until we get bored or we magically find the answers?"

"There's plenty of ways to do research on the road, but I'm not even suggesting that. Look, I'm not saying 'let's go, right this second.' I'm not saying, 'hey, let's drive the whole length of Route 66–'"

Byron gave an exaggerated pout. "You can't, they paved over a lot of it."

"Whatever, I'm not from here, I don't know these things," Ronan said. "We can start small – day trips, or weekends away. I've never visited any part of this country apart from the hospital, the neighborhood around your apartment, and your parents' demonically-possessed mansion. You could take me literally anywhere and I'd still be impressed."

"Hell yeah, you would," Byron snorted, "it's always impressive when I take you." He winked.

"For fuck's sake."

"Exactly."

Ronan shook his head in despair. "Your ego is–"

"Entirely justified."

It didn't help that he couldn't really argue with Byron's assessment of his own prowess.

"Can we get back on topic for a minute, please?" Ronan asked. Byron grimaced a little dramatically but had the decency to nod. "Thank you. Driving that car is tiring for me too. But we can take turns. And we don't have to go far. Let's just get some maps and make some plans – maybe we work up to a big adventure."

He reached out and took Byron's hand across the table again. His fingers were sticky with syrup. It didn't matter.

"That's what I want to do with my life for the foreseeable future."

"Okay. Where do we start?"

Ronan yawned. "Right now there's only one place I want to go. Bed."

"This time *you* read *my* mind."

After a night spent on the chilly asphalt of a parking lot, the bed in Byron's apartment was even more comfortable than Ronan remembered. Or perhaps that was just the added benefit of his new pillow.

Thanks to their carb-heavy breakfast, they'd both slept soundly through most of the day. Byron had woke Ronan near midnight with kisses and the delivery of a pizza that had been stone cold by the time the kisses reached their natural conclusion.

Now they were lounging in the afterglow and finally doing some research.

Beneath his head Ronan felt Byron's ass shake a little as he laughed at something.

"What have you found?" Ronan asked, without looking up from his phone screen. He'd stumbled down a rabbit hole of articles about strange phenomena in Massachusetts.

"It's a one-star review of a romantic but haunted bed and breakfast." Byron cleared his throat and began to read in a pompous voice, "*Too Haunted – my wife and I intended to stay at this hotel for a week to celebrate our twentieth wedding anniversary, however we were forced to leave after only three days by ghostly activity. Every night we were woken up by loud moans and heavy thumping that continued almost until dawn. The website claims that their ghost quietly haunts the corridors but there is clearly something demonic in the honeymoon suite! If you're offered room 202, refuse it unless you want a sleepless night."*

"It's his wife I feel sorry for," Ronan said, once he'd finally stopped laughing. "Let me guess – room 202 is next to the honeymoon suite?"

"Yup."

"I mean, it could be ghosts. If it was demons they'd have complained about the smell." Ronan rolled onto his side, peering past the curve of Byron's shoulder muscles at his phone. The place looked nice. "Where is this bed and breakfast?"

There was a pause as Byron tapped at a navigation app.

"Just outside Atlantic City, so three, maybe four hours depending on traffic," he said. "There's a double Jacuzzi in the room too."

"Oh, now that's appealing," Ronan sighed, rubbing his cheek lightly against Byron's lower back for emphasis. "Even if there aren't any ghosts we can always make the best of a romantic getaway."

Byron shivered a little at the scratching of Ronan's beard across his skin. Over his shoulder Ronan could just see the edge of his grin.

"If there are ghosts, we can see who moans louder."

"I love the way your mind works."

About the Author

G.V. Pearce has appeared in many guises over the years but these days they can most often be found wandering the Yorkshire Dales in search of haunted ruins, or a decent wi-fi signal.

This is G.V.'s first book in the *Eldritch Roads* series, and if their editor has their way it will be followed by two dozen more. In the meantime G.V.'s first novel *Ghost Story*, a Sherlockian mystery-romance, is available in paperback or ebook from Improbable Press.

Find More Supernatural Tales

Improbable Press.co.uk

Former detective Brodie Henshall's Scotland getaway turns into a literal disaster when an earthquake hits the Isle of Skye – crumbling the famous Old Man of Storr right on top of a stranger. Who turns out to have been dead *before* the massive rock fell.

Brodie teams up with local detective Mathias Caradoc, and together they investigate an ever-growing series of supernatural happenings, and start to fall for each other.

Beset by new visions, old witchcraft, and strange phenomena, Henshall and Caradoc must solve a mystery, watch each other's backs, and, ultimately, face the Stag God, in the first novella of J.O. Phael's *Caradoc & Henshall* supernatural mystery series.

John Watson loves his husband, but he'd like Sherlock Holmes to leave this case alone.

They're supposed to be taking a break from London. From work. But then again, when has Sherlock's brain ever taken a holiday? And honestly, the strange disappearance of Gloria Evans bothers them both – though for very different reasons.

Not every one of Sherlock's cases is high stakes. Not every case is a matter of life or death. But sometimes it is.

Do Sherlock Holmes and John Watson have a ghost of a chance in solving what happened to Gloria Evans? Find out in *Ghost Story*, by G.V. Pearce.